Scribe Publications
## THE DAY I KILLED MY FATHER

MARIO SABINO was born in São Paulo in 1962. He is deputy managing editor of *Veja*, Brazil's most influential weekly magazine. His second book, a collection of short stories, *O Antinarciso (The Antinarcissist)*, won the Brazilian National Library's Clarice Lispector Award. He has completed his second collection of short stories, *A Boca da Verdade (The Mouth of Truth)*, and is currently working on his second novel, entitled *O Vício do Amor (Addicted to Love)*.

ALISON ENTREKIN has translated a number of works by Brazilian and Portuguese authors into English, including *City of God* by Paulo Lins and *Budapest* by Chico Buarque, which was shortlisted for the 2004 Independent Foreign Fiction Prize in the United Kingdom. Originally from Australia, she now lives in Brazil.

# the day

# i killed

# my father

## mario sabino

*Translated by Alison Entrekin*

SCRIBE

*Melbourne • London*

Scribe Publications Pty Ltd
18–20 Edward St, Brunswick, Victoria 3056, Australia
50A Kingsway Place, Sans Walk, London, EC1R 0LU, United Kingdom

Originally published in Portuguese as *O Dia em que Matei Meu Pai*
in Brazil by Record 2004
First published in Australia and New Zealand by Scribe 2009
This edition published 2014

Typeset in 11.75/16 pt Adobe Caslon Pro by the publishers
Printed and bound in England by CPI Group (UK) Ltd.

National Library of Australia
Cataloguing-in-Publication data

Sabino, Mario, 1962-

The Day I Killed My Father.

9781922247278 (pbk.)

869.35

scribepublications.com.au
scribepublications.co.uk

*To those who survive*

# Part One

The day I killed my father was a bright day, although the light was hazy, without shadows or contours. Or perhaps it was grey, that shade of grey which even tinges souls that are not usually inclined to melancholy. It's strange that this is the only detail I don't remember; all the others are still vivid. But why does it matter? The frame, that's all it was — the frame. Why try to jolt nature out of its indifference towards us humans? So, let's get to the facts. I killed my father as one would an insect. No, this image is false, since there's usually irritation, if not fear, in such a pedestrian act. I digress — forgive me. It would be more precise to say that I killed my father as one breathes. Steady breathing, that is, requiring no great effort to get air to the lungs.

It was with a blow to the back of his neck and another to the top of his head. He was sitting on his living-room sofa reading the paper as he did every morning before going to the club, where he would swim fifteen hundred metres in forty minutes. An athletic man, my father always sported a tan — the tan of the rich, one of the outward signs of his prosperity. I snuck up from behind, my footsteps muffled by the shaggy carpet. With the first blow his torso shot forward, like someone leaning over to tie his shoelaces. Folded over himself, he received the second blow — the chrism that

3

confirms the baptism. The trickle of blood running from the corner of his mouth; his right hand trembling for seconds before coming to rest, inert, on the ground; the look of fright frozen on his face ... Is my description of the scene satisfactory? I hope it hasn't been too unpleasant; that wasn't my intention.

I leaned the piece of wood against the back of the sofa with a care I now recognise as inordinate (as if the wood were a ritualistic object). I walked around the sofa and, before putting my father back on it, caught sight of the page he'd been reading before he died. It was the adult personals. What had he been dreaming of in his last moment? Aline, the sex kitten with honeyed lips? Milena, the naughty girl who was up for anything? Or the sadistic cousins, who promised to do everything twice? I know I could have omitted this part, but knowing he was interested in ads for prostitutes lends him an endearing humanity. I said 'humanity', but 'weakness' would be more fitting. He was known — respected, in fact — for his power of seduction. My father, until the end I decreed him, had shown he was capable of enchanting women of any age and from any walk of life. It was impossible to imagine him having to pay to go to bed with one. Women — every one he'd had — were crazy about him. Prostitutes are for men like me. Used to be.

I laid my father's body on the sofa and sat on its edge, near his head. I don't know how long I stayed there staring at him, but it was long enough for me to memorise every furrow in his face. When I closed his bulging eyes, his look of fright gave way to a smile. But that may have been my imagination.

4

Then I called the police. 'Come and arrest me,' I said. 'I've killed my father.'

I was five when I saw the ocean for the first time. And it was the ocean that gave me the opportunity to see how much my existence was connected to my father's. Until those distant summer holidays (some thirty years ago), he had simply been an extra in my childhood. Since I was an only child—which I believed to be true until not long ago—I had spent my days enjoying my mother's full-time devotion. She fed my body, nourished my soul, inhabited my dreams. A love story at once unique and yet identical to so many others. In my childish self-centredness, I believed that the intensity of my love, as well as my fidelity, was fully reciprocated. If I could have expressed my deepest feelings at the time, I would have said that I was the creature who had come to put a full stop to lust. A happy ending. I was a dream come true—her ideal, her redemption, her saviour. The truth. But this is, to a greater or lesser degree, everyone's story, isn't it?

That summer's day, the joy of meaning everything to her seemed confirmed by the radiant morning. The sky was a crayon blue … There I go, invoking nature again; forgive me. But it was my desperation, or what it caused, that has kept the day crystal clear in my mind. We arrived at the beach after walking a few blocks from the condominium where my parents had rented a house. Our walk took a while, as I was curious to examine the plants, stones, and insects I found along the dirt road. My father set up the beach umbrella near a stone wall, and my mother and I went to build a sandcastle near the water. After a while, I picked up my pail and waded into the sea. 'I'm going to catch a wave to fill the moat,' I told her.

I had waded a few metres into the shallow water when I saw a minuscule fish swimming between my legs. It occurred to me to catch it in my pail and take it to my mother as a present. I tried to catch it, once, twice, but it managed to escape each time. For a moment I hesitated before continuing my fishing. But the idea of surprising my mother overcame my caution. I followed the fish further into the sea until I found myself chest-deep in water. I had never gone so far out on my own, and wished an adult hand was there to steady me. Where was my mother? 'Mummy!' I cried, looking at the fish, which had come back to play around my legs. When I looked up towards the horizon, a wave big enough to cover me was already looming over my head. I was swept into the roar of the breaking wave. And on that sunny morning, everything went dark.

What's a father for? My analyst … Don't tell me you didn't know? … Yes, I had an analyst, before you came into my life … Or I came into yours, whatever … My analyst used to sit there in silence whenever she heard this question. You know, that rather tragic analyst-silence that sets you at a crossroads, all the paths leading everywhere, which isn't anywhere. Would things have turned out differently if there had been an answer? Anyway, it's too late now. I left the crossroads by a shortcut, that's for sure. Am I mad? Maybe, but madness has given me back lucidity—this lucidity, at least. I've accepted it. Today it is clear to me that, until I bludgeoned him to death, my father's purpose in life was to humiliate me.

The first humiliation he inflicted on me was saving my life that summer morning. The wave crashed down so violently that I passed out. I have nothing to say about the experience in itself, except that to this day it was the only time in my life that I did so. I woke up in a room whiter than this one seems to be. My head was aching, the first in a series of headaches that were to torment me as a child. At the foot of the bed was the familiar sight of my teddy bear. What was I doing there? I turned to look at the window. My father and mother were kissing. And, I can say now, voraciously, urgently, passionately.

I screamed like someone trapped in a nightmare.

My mother ran over and embraced me, crying, 'He's awake!'

Here's a brief summary of what happened. After setting up the beach umbrella, my father was doing his stretches near the sandcastle my mother and I had been building. He always stretched before his morning dip. When he looked up after a sequence of exercises, he saw that I'd gone too far out. Imagining the worst, he threw himself into the sea. Only then did my mother realise she'd been too distracted by the sandcastle (she didn't forgive herself for this for the rest of her life). When I passed out, he was only a few metres from me, and he saved me from drowning. I was taken to hospital, where they said I had concussion. I spent a day sedated so the doctors could assess the extent of the problem. The accident left no physical effects, but to this day I don't know how to swim. I just can't learn. In water, my body is made of lead. The fact that my father was an excellent swimmer gave this inability additional significance.

I'd never seen my parents kissing. Not even hugging. When I was a teenager I discovered that they'd grown apart months after my birth. The real reason was unknown, but family mythology had handed down several versions: my mother had become frigid; my father had taken a lover; her extreme dedication to the baby made him jealous and he'd felt like an intruder; paternity had pushed him into a deep depression. What to believe? Perhaps each of these versions contains a fragment of the truth. And perhaps there isn't actually a whole, solid truth, in which everything fits together perfectly. And perhaps the truth is no more than this: a messy jumble of half-truths.

The interesting thing is that, while my birth drove a wedge between them, my near-death brought them back together. And I was reborn that day so that part of me might die.

Their love was unbearable. After that day on the beach, my father became the strong one and I became the weak one. My mother's caresses seemed like charity compared to what she reserved for my father. When she was with me she was unable to hide her desire to be with him. Her bedtime stories grew shorter. The long sessions of hair-stroking that used to send me off to sleep were replaced with perfunctory kisses. She abandoned me to the threatening shadows in my room. How many times I wanted to cry out! How many ghosts I saw dancing at my window! One of them had rattles for hands. His appearances were announced by the clattering of his rattles. The most torturous thing was knowing they'd come, waiting for them without being able to avoid the wait. I don't believe in other-worldly beings, spirits, tortured souls, or whatever you want to call them. But I believe in these ghosts that tormented me in my childhood. After so many years, fear still prowls around me when they turn out the cell light. It's strange, in my current condition, to be afraid of the dark … This isn't a cell? For me, it is.

At first I tried to come between the happy couple, using everyday ploys which are all described in the literature on psychoanalysis in chapters that deal with the inevitable complex. I got between them so they couldn't hug. I came up with excuses not to leave them alone. But, like I said, I was the weak one. This weakness was to become even more evident on the most terrible night of my life. One of the most terrible nights, that is.

My parents now slept with their door closed. I stayed outside, in the prison of the world. That night, I woke to the sound of the ghost's rattles. The clattering was louder than ever. I tried not to look at the window. Lying face-down against the wall, beneath the covers, I hid my head under my pillow. Useless. Terror often exercises an overwhelming attraction. My resistance broke when, in addition to the rattling, I heard banging on the glass. It was the first time this had happened. So I looked.

There he was, my old acquaintance, dancing in a frenzy. Beside him, however, was a figure I'd never seen before: a boy my own age, kneeling, as if about to be sacrificed. A blue stone shone in one of his hands … What did he look like?

His face was mine.

I leapt up and ran to my mother's door. I stopped in front of it in breathless silence, although I really wanted to bang on it and scream. I stood there for a minute or two, not knowing what to do. I decided to continue when I heard a loud noise coming from my own room. *The ghosts have got into the house*, I thought, petrified. I carefully pushed my mother's door open and went into the walk-in closet. I hesitated before entering the bedroom itself when I saw that the light in the bathroom, on the other side, was on and shining across a part of the bed. But there was no way I could go back—I'd sleep on the floor by my mother's side. It was the only way I'd be safe.

11

I took a few steps forward, and to this day I regret having done so.

The spectacle taking place on the bed was horrible: my mother, naked, was sitting astride an enormous penis. The penis I'd always wanted to see and had always avoided looking at.

## –4–

Forgive me, but none of what I told you yesterday actually happened. That is, it was only partially true ... Up to the vision of the blue stone. How could you have believed that I saw my mother and father having sex? My story was so formulaic, so textbook ... From the look of things, you're an easy girl to fool. Maybe I should devote myself to that from now on—fooling you. It could be my hobby.

Yes, you're right. Even though I invent certain episodes of my history, their essence is immutable; practically Psychology 101 material ... Is that what I wanted to see, deep down? No, not exactly.

What do I make of this attempt to falsify my story? Maybe I want to connect with you. But I don't want any connections at all. None, you hear me? Well, actually, I do ... After all, I agreed to tell you everything that happened, although no one forced me to. What connection might that be? Well, that's something for you to speculate about in some poorly written article.

I am tetchy, I know. Forgive me. I'm tired. I didn't sleep a wink last night. I had a strange dream about the blue stone. I bet your eyes lit up when I said 'dream'. I'm going to satisfy your curiosity, even though our agreement doesn't cover the present.

I was in a dungeon that, as always happens in dreams, wasn't a dungeon, but a hospital. I went down a dark corridor which led to a square area lined with iron doors, where I found a child of about six or seven. The child was wearing one of those little suits that boys used to wear when they received their first communion. His expression was a mixture of sadness, resignation, and perplexity. Beside him was a nurse, who gave me a professional smile. In silence, she led the boy by the arm to the nearest door, opened it, and motioned for him to enter. When he'd gone in, she closed the door. At that instant, I realised the boy was me. I now found myself inside the cell he'd been led into. I was horrified by what I saw around me: the walls were lined from top to bottom with bleeding foetuses. It was no longer a dungeon, but a catacomb. I looked away, towards the door. In it was a tiny barred window, through which the nurse was watching me with her typical nurse's smile. Then she held out a hand through the bars. In it was a blue stone that shone like a fairytale diamond. I woke up right after that, and couldn't get back to sleep.

This blue stone had already appeared in other dreams. I'll make your job easier: my father's eyes were blue. This association was made when it came up in analysis. But, from the look of things, it wasn't … What do you call it, again? Ah, yes, 'processed'.' That's a stone best left unturned.

Anyway, the truth is that I never saw my parents having sex. My nocturnal terrors and my mother's daily demonstrations of love for my father, and vice-versa, were enough to feed my weakness. Until the age of nine, I did everything in my power to sabotage the happy couple's life together. I invented illnesses to keep her away from him at night. I plagued them so much that I managed to play them against one another in arguments about what to do with me. I provoked my father until he threatened to beat me, which earned him sharp scoldings from my mother—and me her affection. Most children use these ruses, I know, but the jealousy and hatred behind them usually remain nebulous. Not in my case, though. I knew I hated my father, and had no remorse about it. I liked it.

When I learned to read, I started using yet another tactic to lash out at the executioner of my childhood illusions and to earn my beloved's attention: intellectual humiliation. Since my father was pretty useless as far as general knowledge went, I took pleasure in showing my mother how much I'd learned in the history books I was now devouring. My little performance always took place at dinnertime, when the three of us were together. Greek mythology, important events in the history of the Roman Empire, memorable World War II battles. The cue for me to start rolling out my repertoire was always a laconic 'Dunno' from my father to something I'd asked him. My mother seemed proud of my erudition because she read widely, and was interested in art and everything else traditionally referred to as the humanities. But my father, to my delight, was unable to hide his discomfort. Little by little, he was also learning to hate me. Proof of this was the torture he put me through when I was seven.

Yes, my father's purpose in life was also to torture me. He never beat me, but he liked simulating fights so he could hurt me. His favourite method was asphyxiation. He'd immobilise me with the weight of his body and only get off when my face started going purple. To make me 'a man', he'd get me into an arm lock and wait until I begged him to stop. Once he broke my finger, which was only diagnosed two days later because he kept insisting that it was nothing and that I was being a 'pansy'. My mother thought it was all normal. 'Boys' games,' she'd say. But nothing hurt me as much as the three words he fired at me one night.

As you know, it's common for children to wonder, at some stage, if they really did come from their parents. This adoption fantasy haunts boys and girls alike, and they will often try to assure themselves of their family identity. In my case, I did it indirectly by asking questions about the circumstances of my birth. I bombarded my mother with questions about the day I was born, the hospital she'd had me in, her first impressions of me—things like that. I also liked to see photos of myself as a baby. This all reassured me, but not enough to erase my doubts. And, whenever I could, I'd trot out my questions again.

It was after one of these question-and-answer sessions

that my father decided to make his move. 'Let me tuck him in,' he said to my mother as he picked me up. When we got to the bedroom, he put me in bed, covered me, and sat down next to me. He stared at me for a few seconds and then, without moving a single muscle in his face, said, 'You are adopted.'

I cried all night long until I heard the first sounds of the morning lashing at the window. My anguish manifested as an asymptomatic fever that increased at nightfall. Without a clear diagnosis, the doctor said I'd caught a virus. My mother tried to comfort me, but I fled her embrace. I came up with excuses and took refuge in my bedroom. I felt betrayed by her. Why hadn't she told me? There was, however, an underlying question, which was impossible for me to formulate at that point: what to do with my love for that woman who was no longer my mother? I could, of course, have asked her if it was true that I wasn't her son. Why didn't I? It was out of resentment (I felt betrayed, as I said), but also for fear of what she might say. I think I was afraid I'd die if I heard her say, 'It's true you're not my son.'

Any other father would have taken pity on me. But not him. On the contrary, he took the opportunity to gloat. At the dinner table, he turned my game around. He provoked me with general-knowledge questions, which I didn't answer. 'Now, now, someone's got the smart-aleck's tongue,' he taunted. My mother begged him to let me be, to which he replied that he was only joking, trying to cheer me up. At one such meal, in the middle of one of his little performances, he said to my mother, 'Can't you see he's acting all la-di-da? Come on, spit it out. What's the capital

17

of Hungary—Bucharest or Budapest?' Angrily, I answered, 'Budapest, you idiot. You'd know if you'd read *The Paul Street Boys*. But you don't read anything. Only Mummy does.' For my pains, I got a glass of water in my face. 'Get out of here before I give you a whipping,' roared my father, while my mother cried, mortified. That same night, my father came into my room and, after lecturing me on the respect that children owe their parents, started to tell me the tale of my adoption. 'The only reason I'm not going to punish you is because I understand how you're feeling about the adoption. You haven't asked for any details, but I'm going to tell you anyway. You're actually the child of a domestic we had the first year we were married. She asked us to look after you for a while, until she got back from holidays, but she never showed up again. She still might come back. But don't worry. Mummy and daddy won't let you go. Goodnight. Sweet dreams, son.'

Can you imagine my terror? No, you can't. No one can.

My anguish lasted about a week. One morning, my father and I were sitting at the breakfast table when, without lifting his eyes from the paper, he said, 'It's interesting how living together can make people alike. Even physically. You, for example, have her eyes. Your mother's. Your eyes are the same; everyone says so. When you were a baby there was no similarity.' He folded the paper, placed it on the table, took a sip of coffee, and only then, after all those gestures, did he look at me. 'We'd best keep this adoption story between us. A father–son thing. A man's thing. Your mother wouldn't understand. It's part of the training you need to learn to deal with life's difficulties. Come here and let me give you a hug.'

My eyes were my mother's; I was no longer in doubt. My eyes …

He'd said that living together made people alike. But he'd also referred to the time when I was a tiny baby. Most adopted children are adopted when they are very small, I know, but that phrase—'When you were a baby'—made me feel certain that I was their natural child and not adopted. It's still a fragile certainty, even though I have become very much like my mother. Could this be through having lived together? But I didn't live with her for very long, when all's said and done …

I let my father hug me, in a mixture of relief and rage, without asking what had led him to torture me like that. It wasn't necessary. It was already clear to me that we were enemies. After the relief and rage came a feeling that could be defined as gratitude. I was grateful to my father for having put an end to my agony, even with all his ambiguity. There's an explanation for this: those who are tortured also feel gratitude toward their torturers when they stop maltreating them.

My tenth birthday party — a big one, which was going to be held at an amusement park — had to be cancelled at the last minute because my mother learned she had cancer. She would be dead in four months. The tumour had started in an ovary, and had spread to her intestine, stomach, and lungs. What have I got to say about it? Well, when she explained her illness to me, she didn't tell me she might die. And, although I watched her waste away, it didn't seem possible that she was about to disappear. She was hospitalised for the last time one morning after vomiting up a smelly, black soup that doctors refer to as faecal matter — the cancer had grown so big that it was blocking her intestine. When she left home, propped up by my father, she said, 'Be happy, son.' And she kissed me on the forehead, a cold kiss. I never saw her alive again.

I was woken in the middle of the night by my aunt, who'd come from abroad to help look after my mother, her younger sister. 'Darling, I need to tell you something,' she murmured. 'What?' I asked sleepily. 'Your mother's gone to heaven,' she answered, her voice faltering.

At that moment, the words 'Your mother's gone to heaven' made no sense at all to me. That's why it took me a while to work out what had happened. When she saw my confounded expression (that was how she described it years later), she used the right words: 'Your mother's dead.'

I'm tired.

I'd like to go back a bit to talk about the effect that my mother's wasting away had on me. Her gauntness, her listless gaze, her white skin, with the pallidness that announces death, her baldness caused by the chemotherapy—to me, this all seemed like a costume that could be taken off at any moment by the woman I loved so much and who seemed so strong to me. It was as if she remained untouched behind that emaciated body. While waiting for my real mother to come back, I avoided the sorry creature who dragged herself through the house and no longer sought my affection. It's strange, I know, that a son as loving as I was could have behaved like that during his mother's illness. But I had no idea she might die, and the fact that she didn't look the same as always left me more perplexed than sad.

It was only that night that sadness caught up with me—or, rather, that I caught up with sadness, because maybe it was me who was behind it. But it was hard to separate sadness from remorse, and my pain grew because I was unable to do so. Why hadn't I hugged her more? Why hadn't I said anything the last time I saw her? I felt like I was the cause of her cancer. In fact, more than that—that I was the cancer. I pulled away from my aunt, who was trying to hug me, and ran to my mother's bed. I wanted to smell her, like little animals do when they look for their mothers who've gone forever … No, that image didn't just come to me now. I'm faithfully reproducing everything that went through my child-mind. At that moment, I remembered the documentaries about baby animals I liked to watch on TV. I always got teary-eyed when I saw them abandoned. If I could find my mother's smell maybe I'd be able to cry. But the tears didn't come. They never came again. I don't remember the last time I cried. I don't know if it was because I was upset, hurt, or had been told off. All I know is that, after I turned ten and everything changed at home because of my mother's illness, I never shed another tear.

With my face buried in her pillow, tearless, I broke into a cold sweat. Then I felt faint. 'I feel dizzy, Aunty,' I said. And at the wake, still reeling, I saw my mother's face — wearing that stupid, beatific smile drawn on by those who prepare the dead — for the last time. Reeling, I watched as her coffin was buried and, reeling, I was patted by people I knew and people I didn't. Still reeling, I glared at my father when he said, 'Now it's just me and you.'

I beg your pardon? Do I still have dizzy spells? Well, in my current state, it's hard to say what I'm feeling. Sometimes I feel as if I'm being swallowed by darkness, while at others it's as if I've lost my individual contours. What do I mean by that? I'll try to explain. Let me see … It's as if the sounds around me were passing through me. They enter through my pores, pass through my body, and carry away what I guess you could call my essence. I feel disoriented, but it's not exactly dizziness or faintness. It's a bit like the feeling described by people who have panic attacks when they find themselves in a crowd. Your body loses its limits, your very substance starts to wane, and it seems like everything is going to melt away, dissolve. To recover, I have to be alone, in complete silence, which isn't easy around here with so many people coming and going from my cell all day long. From my room, I mean.

No, I didn't feel dizzy when I killed my father. Nor did I feel at all faint afterwards. My lawyers said it would have weighed in my favour during the trial; to reinforce what they claimed was a temporary loss of lucidity or some such legal baloney. But I didn't want to lie. At any rate, they managed to do a good job of convincing the different judges along the way that I should be locked up in a place like this rather than a prison. Though I helped quite a lot in that respect, too.

'Now it's just me and you.' Yes, you're right, these are words that precede duels in films. Except that there was never a component of fiction in our clash. It was the most real thing in my life. Now there's nothing that can be done. And perhaps there's nothing more to say either ... I'm tired. My conversations with you every other day wear me out. I think it'd be better if we stopped them ... What? That would put you in an awkward situation? Why should I be considerate with you? I don't really know you. I only know your name—your first name. I don't know where you live, if you're married, if you have kids, if you go to a gym, if you suffer for any reason, how much you earn. Nothing. But you know everything about me—or you think you do. But I don't tell you everything. Not even the file you had access to is complete. No, that's also my tragedy: everything about me is known. I'm a man picked to pieces by analyses, descriptions, comments, judgements. There isn't a soul alive with a more transparent background than mine. Actually, if you have a copy of my hefty court records, you don't really need to be here, hearing it all again ... Yes, that's true, I must admit. As I retell my story, new details emerge. There's one thing that bothers me, though. In spite of all the visibility that my existence has acquired, a part of me remains invisible, obscure, closed up inside itself. Is this what they refer to as soul—the essence that cannot be unravelled, no matter how closely we scrutinise it?

You read that I was writing a book when I killed my father. It's true. I have an unfinished novel on my résumé. I've managed to keep it out of the hands of the law. It does have autobiographical elements, obviously, but nothing about my conflict with my father ... You'd like to read it? I don't know ... The title? *Future* ... What's it about? A guy who's lost, who'd like to make something of himself, and runs into insurmountable obstacles ... What do you mean, 'Is that all?' Don't you think it's enough? My character has philosophical questions, which lead him to choose a certain path. Am I making you curious? I'm afraid you're going to be even more disappointed in me if you read what I wrote. I wouldn't like you to be disappointed in me, you know. I really like your voice, although I don't hear it much ... I'm sorry. I don't mean to embarrass you. So, do you really want to read my book? We'll see ... But, if I say yes, you'll have to agree to one condition—that you will read my book here, aloud, so I can hear it. It'd be an interesting experience for me to hear my words coming from your mouth ... Do you agree to this? I'll consider your request.

I decided to write a book because I was jam-coloured. That was the underlying reason. Before you ask, I'll explain: when I was seventeen, that was how a literature teacher defined me. Jam-coloured. He considered himself to be a bit of a psychic, and liked to categorise people by colour. This game made him popular among the students — especially the boys, whom he appreciated from afar, as an inmate would, poor thing. He'd stare at a student in the face and, after a few seconds, as if he'd seen their soul, would tell them if they were blue, red, yellow, or green. As far as I know, I was the only one to be defined as jam-coloured. He stared at me a little longer than usual, hesitated, then finally delivered his verdict. I was intrigued, and asked him what jam-coloured actually meant, since jam came in a range of colours. He didn't know how to answer.

Are you laughing? Go ahead … After so many years, it's just funny. But I didn't find it remotely funny at the time. To be honest, I still don't find my teacher's description funny. When you're seventeen, you want, above all, to have clear contours, a well-defined colour. And jam-coloured isn't any real colour; it's nothing. It's somewhere between burgundy and brown, I think … At any rate, my teacher wasn't exactly wrong. I really was colourless, and remained so until I killed my father, when I finally gained a colour.

What colour is a patricide? It took me a long time to answer that question. But I did. A patricide is white, all white—the white of the nothing that once was everything. You don't get it? Let me see ... The white of a star that is born, develops, sparks the appearance of a system around it and dies in an explosion that swallows everything around it, and is quickly followed by an incredible concentration of matter that is no longer anything. Just a white spot in space. Colours ... Even my nightmares used to be in colour. With time, black and white took over my dreams, colours became memory—and, from memory, they turned into concepts. The concept of red, the concept of green, the concept of yellow. And the concept of white.

Might I also lose these concepts one day?

As I was saying, I decided to write a book because this undefinable jam colour impregnated my existence until I was an adult. It extended into every corner of my life. My jam-coloured existence was almost completely unreal, and I urgently needed to become real—or to belong to a reality, that is, that bore no connection to that of my perpetual war with my father. It's curious that one might turn to fiction to reach reality, but I think that's how it works for some writers or would-be writers—and I ended up becoming just that, a would-be writer. Many years ago, I watched a re-run of an interview with Clarice Lispector [the Brazilian writer who lived from 1925 to 1977]. Have you read Clarice Lispector? What a silly question; of course you've read Clarice ... How do I know, if you didn't answer? Something about the way you speak makes me assume so.

She's not my favourite writer, but I was quite taken by her persona. Those almond-shaped eyes that seemed to see an invisible world, her crooked fingers, her strange accent with inflections from the Brazilian north-east and the Ukraine. Clarice, in all her humanity, was an other-worldly creature. Anyway, in this TV re-run, at a certain point she said she wrote so as not to die; it was what kept her alive. And between the end of one book and the beginning of the next, she died. That sense of death, uselessness, lack of horizon, disorientation, was what I was feeling at the time, regardless of the fact that I was dutifully completing each stage of life that a man is supposed to. The end of my university years, finishing my Master's in France, moving into a home of my own, getting married—nothing had jolted me out of this frame of mind. My anxiety was like a noise. Sometimes louder, sometimes quieter, sometimes almost imperceptible, but always there, present. After watching the interview with Clarice, I thought that maybe during the writing of a book I'd be able to put it—my anxiety, I mean—on hold. If it all worked out, I could write books back-to-back, and thereby go on living with some pleasure.

Obviously I'd already thought about being a writer before watching the interview. But it was important in helping me decide to shake off my state of lethargy. A brainwave? Yes, a brainwave. I was teaching a few classes at a shoddy university, doing the odd translation, proofing the occasional thesis—so I had plenty of spare time to devote to writing a novel. But I always ended up finding a way to put off sitting down at the computer. I still didn't have enough incentive to turn my paralysing anxiety into stimulating anxiety. Money?

You know my father was rich. Every month he deposited a handsome sum into my bank account, which increased after I got married, seeing as my wife was what you might call high-maintenance, and my father admired her for it ... Yes, being supported by my father was a source of some anxiety. I was just one more whore he paid ... Sorry? I said at the beginning that he didn't sleep with prostitutes? That's true. But that's how I felt—like a whore. Like everyone else who orbited around him.

A few months before I saw the interview with Clarice, I started analysis. I admit that therapy also helped a lot in my decision to write. But maybe my analyst thought that my initiative was just a way of working through the neurosis of the ... that complex ... Why do I avoid talking about the Oedipus complex? Before everything happened, the only reason I didn't mention it was because the name sounded ridiculous to my ears. Perhaps because I'd heard conversations in which people came out with things like 'My Oedipus is affecting my relationship' or 'Your Oedipus is stopping you making the right decisions', with embarrassing ease. After I killed my father ... Well, let's just say I'm over him in such a way (not in a psychological sense, obviously) that an Oedipus complex alone cannot begin to describe my tragedy. It has become too weak an expression. Actually, have you ever noticed how words and concepts are only accurate when defining what happens to other people, never ourselves? Or is this just the impression of one who considers himself superior to others, better than everyone else, even when misfortune befalls him? Did you know my analyst wrote that my narcissism was so monstrous that in

order to differentiate myself from mere mortals, I'd decided
to brand my own story with the myth, becoming it myself.
It seems quite plausible; even so, after that interpretation I
can't help but think of her as a fucking bitch.

–9–

For two years after my mother's death, I went to mass every Sunday. I was taken by an old domestic of ours who thought it was my duty, as an orphan, to pray to God for my mother's soul. The architecture of this church was curious. It was simple outside; imposing inside. It had a main nave and two side aisles. The columns separating them were made of dark marble, with fine Corinthian capitals. The high-altar scenography involved a statue of Jesus on the Cross, with statues of Mary and Mary Magdalene on either side, kneeling, gazing at him. Behind them, a purple curtain, like the ones in opera theatres, provided the backdrop. Above the high altar was a fresco of the Resurrection: Jesus, holding a standard with a cross on it, was levitating over the tomb that had held his body, while Roman soldiers shielded their eyes against the light emanating from the divine spectacle. Next to the high altar was a huge pulpit carved in dark wood, where the priest preached. Opposite it, above the main entrance, was a silver organ, which was only used on special occasions. The side aisles had chapels devoted to different saints, most of whom were Italian, since the church had been financed by Italian immigrants. The altar in the left-hand aisle had a statue of Saint Paul of the Cross, while the right-hand one had a statue of the Virgin Mary.

It was in this church that I had taken my first communion and shat my pants during a school ceremony, the shit seeping through the white knee-highs that were part of my school uniform. Both occasions were branded in my memory, not least for the fact that my father wasn't present at either one. On my first communion, arguing that it was just institutionalised superstition, he spent the day out of town on a friend's farm. My mother was really hurt, but I liked not having him around. I managed to be the centre of attention all day long. As for the school ceremony, I don't remember why he wasn't there. I was relieved he hadn't witnessed my public humiliation—and my mother didn't tell him anything about it, on my insistence ... You think she might have told him without me knowing about it? I doubt it. He would have mocked me. If he didn't, it's because he didn't know.

This old domestic of ours liked to go to church on Sundays because it was an opportunity for her to have some kind of social life. Not that there wasn't any religious sincerity in her habit. There was, and lots of it, as demonstrated by the fervour of her prayers and her room full of pictures of saints. But she didn't hide her happiness at being able to chat with her equals—the absence of which she resented in our oh-so-hierarchical home full of employees who were always being replaced by my father. For this reason, we always arrived at church half an hour early. I took these moments to wander through the church alone, stopping at the chapels with the most shocking paintings and statues. The one that most fascinated me was a statue of Christ dead, lying inside a glass urn. It was in the first chapel of the right-hand aisle, and was always the final destination of my solitary wanderings. The statue only left there when it was carried by the faithful in the Good Friday procession, thereby making the gloomy streets around the church even sadder. I've never seen one of these processions — my father wouldn't allow it — but our domestic's descriptions were so vivid that, in my mind, the scenes took on the contours of something I'd actually witnessed. It's as if I'd personally watched the slow steps of the hooded men in white tunics who carried the dead Christ, and the men who lit the way with torches, and the women who chanted the Lord's Prayer in a lament that could be heard on the top floors of the buildings, although there weren't as many buildings in the neighbourhood back then. I wonder if the procession still takes place. Do you think you could find out for me? Never mind …

The dead Christ statue seduced and terrified me, like a lover who inspires both attraction and repulsion. Alone, standing before the glass urn, I tried to look away, but it was useless. The stigmata on his feet and hands, the blood running from his chest and head wounds, the crown of thorns that still hurt him — all these details mesmerised me. Nothing in the church seemed as alive as that dead Christ, if you will allow me this paradox. I only turned away from the statue when the small bell that announced the start of mass was rung. No, I'm mistaken. I only left when I saw the priests going into the wooden confessionals that stood between the chapels. I liked confessing, so I could take communion afterwards. My sins were always the same four: disobedience, insolence, recalcitrance, and swear words. I was, in fact, obedient, polite, and helpful, and almost never swore. But you had to have sins in order to confess them and then get the communion wafer. Kneeling in the confessional, I'd murmur my sins to the priest, who would absolve me and prescribe my penance: five Our Fathers, five Hail Marys, and three Acts of Contrition. The accounting was always the same for my four sins.

When I left the confessional, I'd head to the pew where our domestic was sitting, kneel next to her, and pray with great concentration. I'd say, 'Forgive me, God, forgive me,' between each of the prescribed prayers and after the mea culpa. After receiving the wafer in the communion ceremony in the last third of mass, I'd go back, kneel again, and say an Our Father and a Hail Mary for my and my mother's souls. The domestic was always moved by the ardour with which I prayed — so much so that she even spoke to my father about the possibility of my becoming an altar boy. 'The boy's blessed,' she said. My father didn't answer, let out a sarcastic guffaw, and ordered her to make coffee. 'I think it's about time she moved on,' he said aloud when he was alone with me in the living room.

Where am I going with this story? Well, I think it's necessary in order for you to understand an important aspect of my unfinished book.

The Sunday before the poor domestic was fired, I made a discovery after mass was over. In fact, that was the last mass I ever attended in my life. It was also the last time I set foot in that church.

Before leaving, the domestic stopped for a quick chat with some acquaintances. Since I wasn't even remotely interested in their conversation, I decided to take another spin through the side aisles of the church. The sound of my shoes made an echo, an effect I emphasised by stomping. Almost automatically, I ended my jaunt at the chapel that held the glass urn with the dead Christ. There was no one around — the group of women were at the entrance near the baptismal font. I was looking at Christ's stigmata, when a thought popped into my head: *It's all a lie. But, if it were true, that loser would have deserved to die like this.*

I started to shake, and broke into a cold sweat. Where had that thought come from, for God's sake? *Christ was a loser! A loser!* The words were now hammering in my brain and, worse, threatening to leave my mouth. Desperate (yes, desperate is the most accurate definition of my state), I ran to the high altar, where there was the statue of the Virgin. I knelt before her, to say however many Hail Marys, Our Fathers, and Acts of Contrition were necessary to atone for my sin. But what happened was even worse. I gazed at the Virgin's face and thought: *This is the pro who bore that loser. And she must be the daughter of another pro, who was the daughter of another pro, who was the daughter of another pro, all the way back to the beginning.*

I fled. I ran into a priest coming out of the sacristy. 'What's the matter, son?' he asked, trying to stop me. I wiggled out of his grasp and headed for the entrance, where the domestic was. I tugged at her hand. 'Let's go! Let's go!' I cried. The terrible thoughts were still echoing in my head: *Christ was a loser! The Virgin was a pro who was the daughter of another pro.* When I got to the square in front of the church, I looked at the façade with its enormous cross and thought: *I'm going to crap all over this bullshit.*

## 10

The first time I ever mentioned this episode was many years later—talking to my analyst, of course. She interpreted it shrewdly, I must say: when I was cursing Christ, I was expressing my unconscious indignation at my own condition as a boy sacrificed by a father who oscillated between irascibility and absence. When I was cursing Mary (of the immaculate conception, no less), I was expressing my anger, also unconscious, at the mother who had abandoned me and who, at the same time, occupied my entire existence.

I wish I'd had an analyst at that moment in my life. Because, after what happened, I began to believe I was the Antichrist: the Beast that had come to destroy the world. At the same time, a part of me believed the opposite—that it was just a test of my infinite faith. And for this reason I prayed, and prayed, and prayed. I prayed every time the thoughts popped into my head, whether I was at home or in public. When they appeared in the presence of other people, I prayed in a way that they wouldn't notice. I even developed a technique for making the sign of the Cross in slow motion, so to speak, so no one would catch on. Hail Mary always came after Our Father. I read the Hail Mary in Latin in an old missal I found among my mother's belongings. I memorised it and started reciting it in Latin because it

*36*

seemed more sublime and, therefore, more effective. *'Ave Maria, gratia plena, Dominus tecum, benedicta tu in mulieribus et benedictus fructus ventris tui, Iesus. Sancta Maria, Mater Dei, ora pro nobis, peccatoribus, nunc et in hora mortis nostrae, Amen.'*

The anxiety instilled in me by the certainty that I was the Antichrist was to last quite a while. It dissipated slowly, and an important determinant in its erasure was finding out that the Romans used to curse God and the Virgin Mary. For me, the Roman blasphemies represented liberation. *'Dio cane.'* *'Porca Madonna.'* These expressions still sound like poetry to me. It was because of them that I started studying Italian.

Do I believe in God? I could quote Woody Allen: 'To you, I'm an atheist; to God, I'm the Loyal Opposition.' At any rate, knowing of my childhood religious experience is essential for you to be able to understand one of the main aspects of my unfinished book. I wanted to understand how Evil was born in our souls. Because that was my frightening discovery that day, as I later managed to articulate: I, a mere child, was already filled with incommensurable Evil.

My analyst's explanations, I know. Shrewd, but partial. But they only explained the triggers for something that I believed (and still do) was pre-existent ... Have I found an answer to my philosophical question? I have a few theories on the subject, but I'd rather leave them for later. There's no rush. I've got plenty of time on my hands. Actually, it's the only thing I have got.

## 11

Here's the file containing *Future*. I've decided to bring forward the reading for three reasons. First, I miss my characters—yes, 'miss' is the right word. Second, I'm anxious to hear your opinion about the book. Isn't it curious that I barely know you and that I already need your opinion? Last, I think *Future* will help you understand some of my processes. Just some, mind you.

The main condition for me to let you read it, I repeat, is that you do so aloud. I don't think it should take more than four sessions to read. There are other conditions. You can't take the file home. At the end of each session, I'm going to check the number of pages in it. Please excuse my lack of trust, but I wouldn't like people I don't know to have access to my book. Read slowly, please, and don't try to give the characters different voices. I detest those kind of theatrics. Last of all, there are to be no comments during the reading. Nor do I want to hear your observations after each session. You'll read it, then leave, in silence. We'll only discuss it when you've got to the end of the book. Do we have an agreement?

It will be a pleasure to hear what I wrote coming from your mouth.

# Future
## (a novel)

# I

When he read in the paper that light pressure applied to the earlobe could bring on a sudden heart attack, Antonym became suspicious of Bernadette. After all, it was a more subtle method than pouring molten lead into a victim's ear. He saw the article—of dubious scientific quality—as a kind of confirmation. Not just of the motive behind some of his wife's caresses, but also of the theory he'd been nurturing. One day, while waiting for the bathroom to be vacated, a strange matinal mosquito was droning at the entrance to his left ear. At any other time, Antonym would have merely grumbled and swatted the air. But at that hour of the day, when a healthy man has his batteries fully charged, the drone of the insect inspired a quick, though not unreasonable, formulation. After squishing the mosquito against the wall, Antonym realised that it was through their ears, rather than their eyes, that men were seduced. The ear canal connected a man's body and spirit. Caress the eardrums of the most mediocre of beings with words of praise, and he will believe himself to be a wise man; nibble, even just slightly, the earlobe of a wise man, and he is reduced to nothing. Armed with this principle, one could even write, for example, an essay on the harmful aspects of constructive criticism. But Antonym would never do that. He would be caught up in ordinary events that would lead to the extraordinary.

It was nothing more ordinary than a marriage break-up. The relationship had lasted ten years, and would have lasted even longer had Bernadette not plucked up courage and decided to leave, after giving him a long and civilised explanation of her decision.

'I need to be around normal people,' she said in conclusion, before picking up her bags, which were already packed, and going to stay with a girlfriend from work.

The sterility of the scene made Antonym proud. His wife had perfected the ability to control noisy reactions.

'Can I ask you one last thing?' asked Antonym.

'?'

'Did you ever think of killing me?'

Bernadette got into the lift.

# II

The change in Antonym's marital life had an immediate effect on his work. He was unable to come up with enough witty ideas to maintain a good flow of opinionated articles, and his reporting became substandard — even for the third-rate newspaper he worked on, he was forced to admit. His lack of productivity allowed the editor to start detecting lumps in his velvety style, which up until then had been a source of pride for the editor, who believed he had 'discovered the kid'. Whenever he heard him trot out this phrase, it struck Antonym that editors-in-chief were like pimps — always keen to find new talent. It was a shame that that was a cow he couldn't milk any more.

'An article in the first person, Antonym? That's not done in contemporary journalism.'

'Antonym, please go lighter on the "howevers". Your texts are full of crutches.'

'Listen, Antonym. Why don't you use the first person? It's more contemporary.'

'A crutch wouldn't be so bad here, Antonym.'

'I think you should have some time off to reflect on life, Antonym. No hard feelings, OK?'

Antonym was out of the game. Since he'd made countless enemies on all the other newspapers and magazines, he wasn't likely to find work again on a big publication.

*Well, at least a lot of people will be happy now,* he murmured to himself, as he closed his car window in the face of a kid begging for money. *No self-indulgence, no indulging others. No hard feelings, OK?* That was how he had to be.

*In theory, it's possible to love thy neighbour. But from a distance. Close up, it's almost impossible.* He remembered that this was what Bernadette had always said whenever she saw him cursing the vagrants that had taken over the city.

Before he went home, it occurred to him to call someone who could keep him company during his first dinner as an unemployed person. And it was only then, and not without some perplexity, that Antonym understood in reality (which is quite different to understanding in theory) that he had been isolated for years. He had delegated the job of making contact with the outside world to Bernadette, which had meant only going out with her friends and workmates. His own social life was restricted to his work, which gave the term 'social life' far too narrow a meaning. All he had left was enemies. But even they were distant rather than close. Because there were bosom enemies (with whom one could seek reconciliation any time, given the fact that they used to be friends before the fight that caused the falling out), and there were distant enemies. With these, the confrontation generally took place before there could be any kind of friendly exchange or recognition of like-mindedness. Underpinning them might be a quick comment to a third party, a funny look, or a difference of opinion of little relevance on an equally unimportant subject. Since the animosity was established right at the outset, distant enemies were eternal.

You couldn't reunite what had never been united.

Without company, Antonym ended up at the refuge of the solitary: a luncheonette. At a luncheonette, even one with tables instead of a counter, you could eat alone without attracting the pity of those who were accompanied—which wasn't possible in a restaurant. Solitude in a luncheonette always seemed circumstantial, or even preferable for clients who came alone. Quick and bland, like the meals served in such places. This image of being in a state of desired solitude could also be emphasised by reading a magazine.

From that night on, Antonym started spending a considerable amount of money on magazines that really didn't interest him. However, it wouldn't be long before he missed the time when he didn't have friends—or when his enemies were distant.

# III

'Is this right?'

'What?'

'The name on your ID here.'

'Believe it or not, it is. The registrar was a bit out of it and typed an extra "m".'

'Your dad could have fixed it. Or you.'

'True, but I kept Antonym. I've thought about correcting it, but this is a country of even weirder names ... Does it bother you?'

'Why should it bother me?'

'What's your name?'

'Bernadette.'

'That's funny.'

'What?'

'I've always had the impression that there was an "r" missing in Bernadette. That the right spelling should be "Bernardette". You know, when I was a child, I got it into my head that I should be a devotee of the saint. I saw a film about her that had a big effect on me.'

'I really liked the Infant Jesus of Prague.'

'The one with the fingers.'

'Yes.'

'I have something extra, and you seem to be missing something.'

He was going round and round in lethargic circles, reliving his first conversation with his ex-wife, but this was shattered by the sound of a car alarm. Silence had abandoned the world once and for all. Startled by his racing heart, and the bitter taste of barbiturate-induced sleep, he got up. Antonym's intention, in deciding to take this kind of medication regularly, hadn't been to escape his crisis; rather, it had been to put off dealing with it. Abolish, eliminate, cancel all and any drama of existence; reduce life to a white square on a white background—that was his motto.

When he opened the window, and the white of the bedclothes blinded him, he thought he'd achieved his objective, without realising that the daylight was merely blotting out his soul, hiding the ghosts that inhabited the folds of his messy sheets. With a stupid smile, he scratched his big toe, and headed for the bathroom.

The illusion only lasted a minute. The maids' symmetrical tidying caused him discomfort for the first time. Was Bernadette gone forever? With her knickers hanging in the shower, the cabinet drawers half-open, the uncapped eau de cologne. He'd been vegetating in solitude for months. Antonym gazed at himself between the specks of toothpaste on the bathroom mirror. He'd never asked himself: *Who am I?* Rather, he'd asked: *Is that really me?* It was as if the face he saw masked an unfathomable essence that couldn't be recognised in his features, gestures, emotions, and thoughts. And the terror of this brief lucidity killed him a little.

His own Pontius Pilate, he rinsed his hands and eyes. While he was on his way to the kitchen, the telephone rang.

'Antonym?'

'Yes?'

'It's Hemistich.'

'It's been donkey's …'

'I know, I reckon it's been, what … eight years since we last saw each other?'

'Something like that.'

'It's hard to be your friend. You don't call anyone; you always have to be called.'

'I know, that's just me.'

'And here I am once again. Do you know why? Because you're worth it.'

'I hope to let you down.'

'You're worth it.'

'My phone number, how'd you …'

'Bernadette. I ran into her at a dinner. A work thing, I think.'

'You, at one of those dinners?'

'It was at my restaurant.'

'…'

'Hello?'

'I'm here … Your restaurant?'

'There are those who call it a steakhouse. Let me give you the address.'

Hemistich remembered in detail things that everyone else had forgotten. Figures of speech, for example. He didn't need to look in a dictionary to know what 'anastrophe' meant. This made him self-assured. Poet, writer, translator, editor, Master of Philosophy—the biographical footnotes of his articles varied according to need. They contrasted with his fidelity to certain stylistic additives and lubricants in his musings on everything. But the great feat of his career had been the timely domestication of his caustic sense of humour. When he was still young he had almost lost everything after having called a well-known concrete poet '(in)significant'. He was funny and a good conversationalist, but too intense. Hard to live with. He managed to be eternally surrounded by friends, due to the fact that they were never the same ones.

Antonym was shocked. Hemistich Borba the Second, the quintessential Brazilian intellectual, had ended up running a steakhouse.

# IV

The transience of his desire had found a golden mean in the price of satisfying it. Besides, he wasn't in a position to spend a lot. He left her 'come again' behind, and he took the lift down, buried alive. In those days so predictable in their misery, he had clung to routine, discipline, schedules. His regular weekly hour with prostitutes was part of this scheme.

He hesitated briefly at the door of the building. Noticing a vagrant on his left, he turned right. The cathedral loomed before him—an insect with gothic antennae and a rotten apple on its back in the guise of a dome. The stench of urine and fried food rose up from the Portuguese mosaic pavement. Before climbing the stairs, he freed himself from the gypsy woman intent on reading his palm, dodged the man selling limes, and pushed away the street kid tugging at his pants. The inside of the church wasn't much different from the reality around it. While beauty hinders asceticism, so does ugliness. Antonym thus experienced no elevation, inner peace, or reconciliation with the human race in the time he sat there. It was just cooler.

A priest came out of a door next to the high altar, and approached him. Antonym stood up. Was it possible?

'Father Farfarello …'

Domenico Farfarello had been his grammar teacher at school. Short and bald, with cerulean-blue eyes and an aquiline nose, he used to spend a considerable amount of time in front of the mirror, rehearsing expressions that would inspire fear in lazy students, like a Caligula of the education system. At least, this was the rumour at the school run by Italian monks that Antonym had attended.

'So it is you, Antonym! What a nice surprise! It was God who guided my eyes to the pew you were sitting on. I haven't seen you since …'

'… Since Monsignor Salviati's funeral.'

'Salviati, a good servant of God … "Remember you will die".'

'Remember you will die.'

The old ecclesiastical expression that Salviati had loved made them laugh.

'How are you, Antonym?'

'I'm not sure, Father.'

'That's the right answer, son. I have a feeling I was placed in your path to help you.'

'To help me …?'

'To help you.'

'I don't think it would hurt to talk to you.'

'Why don't we go into the sacristy?'

'No. Wouldn't you rather have lunch with me?'

'Is that an invitation?'

'Of course.'

They chose a small restaurant, already half-empty at that hour.

'My marriage is over and I was fired. That's it in a

nutshell. All very banal, I'm afraid.'

*'I guai vengono bensì spesso, perchè si é dato cagione.'*

*'Ma la condotta più cauta e più innocente non basta a tenerli lontani.'*

*'Però quando vengono, o per colpa o senza colpa, la fiducia in Dio li raddolcisce, e li rende utili per una vita migliore.'*

'Manzoni would be a checkmate, Father Farfarello, if I weren't an atheist.'

'Not even the Devil is an atheist, son. If you were really an atheist, you wouldn't be discussing your concerns with a priest.'

'Your order, if I'm not mistaken, practises exorcism. That must be fun. It's even become a spectacle for television.'

'Don't underestimate the Devil. He is part of God and was born of His boredom, which survives inside each and every one of us. How many err just to escape their own routines? Most, to be honest. For this reason, too, God is able to forgive. He himself sinned when He gave in to boredom and created Evil, thus becoming the Creator of sin.'

'That's heresy.'

'No, far from it. God sinned and, in this manner, created sin, because it was part of His plan. And the boredom that moved

---

\* Father Farfello and Antonym are exchanging lines here from the famous Italian historical novel *The Betrothed* by Alessandro Manzoni (1827): 'Troubles certainly often arise from occasion afforded by ourselves; but the most cautious and innocent conduct is not enough to keep us from them; when they come, whether by our own fault or not, confidence in God alleviates them, and makes them useful for a better life.'

Him was another of His creations: something we mortals are able to understand, bearing in mind that not everything that stems from the divine will is within our grasp.'

'These theological somersaults should be an Olympic sport, don't you think? But no one can break the record of Saint Augustine, who invented Original Sin. It was him, wasn't it?'

'Do you know the basis for original sin, son?'

'I'd like to know.'

'Augustine saw sexual motivation in Adam's fall. It was carnal concupiscence that led him to sin. And this sin is repeated every time a man and a woman make a child. Because, in order for there to be birth, there must first be the same carnal concupiscence that was Adam's undoing. The concupiscence that means selfish desire. The Bishop of Hippo didn't invent original sin; he merely revealed it by the grace of God.'

'As I was saying, Saint Augustine is unbeatable. Actually, the fact that he was so extraordinary ... Africa in the fifth century must have been pretty boring. Maybe he started developing theological systems to escape the dreariness around him.'

'Don't confuse things, Antonym. Boredom never moves great men. What propels them is the Idea—which is the same as the Absolute, the unity of subjectivity and objectivity. And what are these concepts if not a philosophical expression of God in all His plenitude?'

'That's the Hegelian right-wing point of view. For the left, that's not the way it works. And the Hegelian left won, father. At least in that, the left won.'

'One must choose a side, son. And I am always on the side of those who have faith in God, even if they've been defeated. Have you read Hegel, son?'

'Very little. I edited the cultural pages of the newspaper I worked on. Hegel in a newspaper, imagine …'

'Anyway, it is God who leads great men to achieve their feats. But never through boredom; rather, through the desire to know God.'

'Isn't it ambition that moves them?'

'Even the personal ambition of great men obeys His plan. Come with me to the sacristy after lunch. I'm going to give you a text by Hegel that I think is very enlightening — although, as a priest, I cannot agree with the Hegelian conclusion that the destiny of all religion is atheism.'

'Well, well. So Hegel really was left wing …'

'Such sarcasm, Antonym. Don't you know philosophers can speak truths without arriving at the Truth? Many get lost along the way.'

'And what about lies? Could they serve as the basis for the Truth?'

Farfarello smiled.

'Antonym, you have yet to grasp the full extent of what you just said merely to be ironic. Let's go, I must be quick.'

*A full day, this one*, thought Antonym. *I fucked a whore, chatted with a priest, and am about to go home with a piece of German philosophy tucked under my arm.*

# V

Every so often, Antonym tried to digest some late-afternoon melancholy with a packet of cornstarch biscuits. He used these moments to make more or less free associations. Any old fact could spark a run. One of the sequences he'd been most chuffed with was inspired by a stumble:

*I tripped and almost fell. If I'd fallen, I would have hurt myself. If I'd hurt myself, I'd be resting in bed. A doctor would come to examine me and give me medicine. Many ancient medicines were made with Eastern drugs. According to Aristotle, the winds are born in the East. Aristotle was the teacher of Alexander the Great. Alexander the Great was lord of the world. The Greeks believed the world was held up by Atlas. Atlas was strong. Strength is symbolised by columns. Columns hold up buildings. Buildings are made by labourers. Labourers are directed by engineers. Engineers work from architects' sketches. Sketching is part of painting. Painting is an art. There are seven liberal arts. Seven is the number of sages who studied eloquence. The goddess of eloquence is Minerva.*

A week after his meeting with Farfarello, Antonym was munching on cornstarch biscuits while making a series of associations that, having started with scouring powder, had already reached superconductors. But he didn't get to what might have been the end of this chain of thoughts.

'I'm so useless. Bernadette was right to leave me.'

Antonym left the packet of biscuits in the kitchen and went to the bedroom. The text Farfarello had given him had been lying on the nightstand for a week—and he hadn't read it.

'Would Hegel have made associations as banal as mine?'

Antonym decided to take the priest's advice to read Hegel's text. It was a compilation of phrases by Hegel that summed up the notion that all great men in history were propelled by the World Spirit, despite the fact that their actions appeared to stem, even in their own eyes, from personal ambitions alone. Such great men—who could be called heroes—were capable of perceiving what needed to be done in their era and, consequently, of revealing the Truth that inhabited all human beings, but to which the majority did not aspire. They had often been warned to proceed with caution along the way, but had pushed on regardless. And, thus, these great men had ended up being followed by those who saw them as the incarnation of their own desires and their own souls.

Of all the quotes, one stuck in Antonym's head: 'The courage of truth, faith in the power of Spirit, are the first conditions of philosophy. Man, because he is Spirit, can and must consider himself worthy of everything that is most sublime. He can never overestimate the greatness and power of his Spirit. And if he has this faith, nothing will be so hard and unyielding as not to reveal itself to him.'

It was already after 9.00 p.m. when Antonym went to meet Hemistich.

# VI

A sculpture of a white steer with golden horns loomed over the entrance of the The Bullseye. Beneath it was a marble plaque with the following inscription:

*I will destroy the wisdom of the wise,*
*and the intelligence of the intelligent I will reject.*
*Where is the wise man? Where is the scholar?*

'How many will be dining with you, sir?'
'Hemistich is waiting for me.'
'May I have your name?'
'I'd rather keep it, if you don't mind.'
'?'
'Antonym.'
'One moment, sir.'

He'd expected a steakhouse that looked like a refectory—with colonial décor or something of the sort—and had found instead a very peculiar restaurant. The first room was a bar clad in dark wood with panels of bullfighting scenes on the walls. The barmen and waiters moved around silently, and the usual sound of glasses and bottles was almost non-existent.

'A dry martini, please.'

As Antonym sipped his martini, he took a closer look at the drawings. Men and bulls clashed with joyous expressions on their faces. In one scene, a bullfighter, about to be gored, had the transfigured look of one on the verge of orgasm.

*Funny*, he thought. *It reminds me of Bernini's* Ecstasy of Saint Teresa.

'Do you like it?' asked Hemistich.

'It's strange in this context, like the inscription over the steakhouse door.'

'Actually, this is more than a steakhouse.'

'Right, it's a new concept in steakhouses, as a publicist would say.'

'Go ahead, joke. I don't care.'

'I'm sorry, Hemistich. I shouldn't be talking like this to the guy who's going to provide me with a free meal. I'm impressed by your steakhouse, or whatever you want to call it. Seriously. Where'd you come up with the money?'

'Let's just say by using some relatively emotional blackmail. Come to the dining room.'

A three-by-fifteen-metre corridor led from the bar to the dining room. Three wall lamps on each side shed yellow light on the people walking through it. Over the dining room door, an enormous Minotaur grinned down at passers-by.

When he entered the dining room, Antonym gulped. On every wall there were scenes of satyrs and nymphs indulging in orgies of food and sex. On the floor were mosaics depicting food leftovers: olive pips, fruit peels, chicken bones, fish skeletons, hunks of meat.

'Surprising? Weird? I know it's hard to choose the right adjective. But I'd say, "Appropriate." This place was designed to celebrate the triumph of the senses over reason. See how relaxed everyone is? Let's sit in that corner. Another dry martini? Risério, two more.'

'So she came here.'

'Bernadette? She really liked it. But the décor was different then.'

'You mentioned relatively emotional blackmail.'

'That's how I got the money.'

'Your intellectual work, of course, wouldn't have paid for all this.'

'I burned everything I ever wrote. I also torched my library.'

'You did what?'

'One thing at a time. First, the blackmail. The wife of a political candidate. Quite pretty. Anyway, I had an affair with her, and I documented it.'

'I'm speechless.'

'I had to truly live. I had to live the truth.'

'Hang on. What, pray tell, is the truth?'

Hemistich smiled.

'Remember Augusto?'

'Of course.'

'He asked the same thing.'

'And what was your answer?'

'I didn't have an answer at the time. But Augusto ended up discovering his own truth — which, from a certain perspective, is everyone's truth.'

'How is he?'

'He killed himself.'

'What?'

'After slashing his wife's throat.'

'He lost it …'

'He left me a letter. A kind of poem, actually. I know it off by heart:

*From tongue to blade, unrestrained. With a swift slash, I gash my beloved's throat. And, among such vocal cords, I seek the words that once filled my ears with tenderness, don't find them, and wonder where they are.*

'It was premeditated?'

'He wrote it after he killed her. The paper had bloodstains on it.'

'Is that the answer? Desperation?'

'To act on impulse, the purest expression of the senses.'

'Death.'

'Death is a contingency.'

'Not your own, you callous prick. I'm hungry.'

'There it is!'

'What?'

'The key to my truth. Let's to the feast, *monsieur*.'

'Let's.'

And that's what they did. And that's how it was to be. Blessed were those called to the supper of Hemistich.

In Antonym's memory, the orgy of rump steaks, porterhouses, t-bones, tenderloins and sirloins, accompanied by an array of perfectly cooked vegetables, seemed like an hallucination. To accompany the banquet was a wine that, from the very first glass, heightened his senses, drove away his anxiety, and made time pause. Meat, wine, meat, wine:

a steady flow of waiters presented oblations with reverence, as if they were serving the lords of the world. All notion of time slipped away. Had it been three, four hours? Impossible to tell. Hemistich was transformed.

'Such is the mystery of faith! Which has been revealed by me, only me! Music incarnate! Where is it?'

At the next table, a group of inebriated Germans stood and began to sing the national anthem — 'Deutschland über Alles'.

Hemistich cackled with laughter.

'Not that, no!'

The dining room was stormed by twenty musicians in colourful clothes and shiny adornments, carrying strange percussion and wind instruments. They played an oriental-sounding melody and sang in an indecipherable language. Then twelve dancers appeared — four brunettes, four blondes, and four redheads. Wearing transparent clothes that provided glimpses of perfect contours, they swayed and gyrated between the tables, occasionally making the high-pitched sound that Muslim women make on festive occasions and when they're mourning.

'Touch the women, Antonym. Go ahead. Come here, my lovely. I want my friend to run his hands over you. Look how smooth she is, Antonym, so soft ... Not silk, not satin. There's nothing nicer to the touch than skin like this. *Parlez, mes mains, pour moi.*'

The room was now spinning around Antonym. A light perfume wafted not only into his nostrils, but into his pores. It was as if there was no longer a barrier between outside and inside, between him and his companions in revelry.

'One body, one soul!'

Hemistich was dancing on the table.

A lysergic effect rippled out in all directions, and the satyrs and nymphs peeled off the walls, and joined the dancers and musicians. In sassy voices, the satyrs sang a song with just one verse:

*Queasy, I vomit*
*a leftover shred,*
*love, eternal dreaming*
*multiplied.*

One of them (or was it Hemistich?) brought his ugly face close to Antonym's.

'Nature, if you are neither mother nor stepmother,' he said, 'if human adventures and misadventures matter not to you (as you have affirmed more than once), all we can do, then, is writhe in your cornucopia, in the hope of a metaphysical echo, or ignore such indifference, and enjoy the mysterious pleasures of existence ...'

'Echoes of Leopardi ... I once read Leopardi ... How I love Bernadette! Maybe if I wore clothes in happy colours, like these musicians ... She got tired of asking. A yellow shirt, a cloud in trousers ... No, I'm not sad. The nostalgia of my shipwrecked love offers so many possibilities. Everyone's fucking. I want to, too, but I don't know if I can ... What did you put in this food, Hemistich? What did you put in this wine, Hemistich? Hemistich, where are you? Where is the wise man? Where is the scholar? Bernadette!'

Antonym cried out, and everything went black.

# VII

'Hi, remember me?'

Antonym examined the discreet crow's-feet that belied her youthful appearance.

'I have to admit I don't.'

'It's Kiki. We went to school together.'

'Oh, right, Kiki. But where are we, Kiki?'

'In Hemistich's office. You passed out last night, and we brought you here.'

'We? Were you in the restaurant?'

'I arrived at the end of the party. I haven't seen anyone from our class for ages … We should get everyone together every now and then, shouldn't we? I always read your articles. I don't understand much, but I generally like them. You were always good at writing …'

'I don't write any more.'

'You're kidding!'

'Let him be, Kiki.'

'Ah, come on, Hemistich. You're always giving me a hard time. I'm going to give you my card, Antonym. Give me a call, OK? You're looking hot. *Ciao*.' As he watched Kiki's arse moving away, Antonym thought how embarrassing it was to be part of certain people's pasts.

'Do you know Kiki?'

'Yeah. We went to school together.'

'Top-notch pussy.'

'A bit past her prime.'

'But she's still a babe. And the best thing is she loves to fuck.'

'This is starting to sound like something out of a porn flick. That was wild, last night. Is it always like that at your steakhouse?'

'Let's just say it was a special night, in your honour.'

'Was it like that for Bernadette?'

'Of course not. She had an absolutely normal dinner.'

'I'm curious. Why did you get into this business?'

'It's a long story. I'm not sure you're up to hearing it now.'

'I'm fine. Go ahead.'

'You probably aren't aware of it, but I fell into a deep depression two years ago. My intellectual career wasn't going anywhere—except to debates on Byzantine topics and to the beds of post-grad lit students—and even that had lost some of its thrill. I felt lethargic; it was hard to get out of bed in the morning, and I was plagued by thoughts of death. Anyway, the symptoms of depression are well known. I went to a psychiatrist, who gave me one of those new drugs. I got better enough to realise that my existence had been a series of mistakes up to that point. If I'd kept going like that, the most I could aspire to was a fifteen-second obituary on educational TV to the sound of a classical guitar ... Have you ever noticed that behind every TV news story about culture, there's always a guitar being strummed? But it wasn't the need for recognition that bothered me the most. I'd stopped seeing any sense in my writing — and in the writing of others. I needed a life.'

'That's not much different from how I feel at the moment.'

'I kind of figured you weren't OK. That's why I called.'

'So, like Paul on the road to Damascus, you had a vision and discovered that you needed to have your own steakhouse.'

'Why the sarcasm?'

'It's a professional vice, as well as a self-defence strategy.'

'Well, anyway, one afternoon, which stretched out before me like all of my afternoons as an idle intellectual, I was taking a shower with my body on automatic pilot — hands, arms, and legs, performing the sequence of obligatory movements that makes one shower exactly the same as all others. We're never further from ourselves than when taking a simple shower, haven't you noticed? But this one was different. As I was soaping up the soles of my feet, I felt, as if for the first time, how soft they were. This fact, which had never been so clear to me, startled me. Startled? No, it frightened me. My feet were like those of a newborn. It wasn't possible that they belonged to a thirty-six-year-old man. They were out of keeping with my receding hairline, my sarcasm.

'Anyhow, that same day, I went to have lunch with a brother I hadn't seen for a while. I led the conversation towards our similarities and dissimilarities (to be honest, I don't think one talks about anything else with siblings), and I started saying how ugly our family's feet were, with crooked toes and everything. I went on so much about it that he took off his shoes to examine his own feet. That was what I'd wanted. My heart started racing when I saw them: my brother's feet had hard, rough, calloused soles. I expressed my perplexity at this difference. He smiled, and said, "What do you expect, Hemistich? You were always cooped up, reading. You didn't play barefoot like I did."

'That banal observation, one that I'd heard all my life, suddenly struck a deep chord. I went home less depressed than ashamed. Yes, I was really embarrassed, filled with the shame of one who finds himself naked in a crowd. Proud Hemistich, arrogant Hemistich, was a coward. My intellectual life meant the opposite of what I'd thought. Ever since I was a child, books hadn't helped me know the world; rather, they'd kept me from it. Through them, I realised, I'd kept reality at bay, or adapted it to my own narrow parameters, which, in the end, is the same thing. I preferred reading the description of a landscape to actually seeing it. I preferred reading about love to feeling it. I preferred reading about pain to feeling it. And, to hide my weakness, I used knowledge like a whip on anyone who dared get close to me. My learning—which, at the end of the day, wasn't so great and for which the word "learning" seemed like over-sized clothes—only served to inspire fear. Nothing more than fear. It had never made me happy, or led anyone to see new aspects of the world.'

Antonym was unable to suppress a laugh.

' "See new aspects of the world." That's a good one, Hemistich. Do you know what that is? Educator? Baloney. I've interviewed a few, and they always say the same thing: "To educate is to help people see new aspects of reality with a critical perspective."'

'Did I say anything about a "critical perspective?"'

'No, but it would complement it well.'

Hemistich got up and went over to the window, which looked on to what seemed to be an inner courtyard. Antonym took the opportunity to examine his friend's office. The walls were completely naked and light blue, like a police station. Next to the window was a heavy desk in dark timber decorated with marquetry, like the high-backed chair behind it. Two lower chairs for visitors completed the arrangement. On the table, a small, carefully stacked pile of papers and a chrome pencil holder only highlighted the lack of clutter. The sofa on which Antonym had woken up stood against the wall opposite the desk. It was covered in black leather, and was brand-spanking new. In front of the sofa, a centre table on a white rug held some magazines and newspapers, also stacked with the same fastidiousness. The publications were dated from the previous week, which reinforced the impression that the room wasn't used very much. *Maybe it's just where Hemistich brings his pussy for the kill*, thought Antonym.

After remaining quiet for a few minutes, Hemistich came away from the window.

'Could it be that we're wrong about you, Antonym?'

'We're wrong?'

'That I'm wrong, I mean.'

'Most probably, yes. My mission on Earth is to disappoint.'

Hemistich walked over to Antonym and looked straight into his eyes, as if searching his retinas.

'No, I'm not wrong. There's something in you that begs to be set free.'

'You're freaking me out, Hemistich. Someone stared at me like that last night, before I passed out. Was it you?'

'No. Do you want me to go on with my story?'

'Please do. It *begs* to be told.'

'You must be asking yourself whether I'd never noticed my limits before then. Yes and no. I'd sensed my cowardice, but intellectual arrogance is peculiar: we are only able to be arrogant with others when we are arrogant enough with ourselves. The right amount of arrogance is that which leads us to believe that we make a difference. After the revelation that I was really just a big farce (because it really was a revelation), I started taking a closer look at the intellectuals around me. They were mirrors of my fragility. It became glaringly obvious to me that, even when armed with total arrogance, they always found a way to avoid straightforward statements and original reasoning. Their articles and essays were amphibological, so to speak; full of emergency exits, of which the most common were the expressions "to a certain extent" and "so to speak". Have you ever noticed how intellectuals overuse them? Much more than stylistic crutches, they're existential ramparts.

'These discoveries were, obviously, followed by the question: What to do? Put a distance between myself and my peers and go to live in another city, where I could reconstruct myself? Vulgar avoidance: I'd just be sweeping my problem under the carpet. I fell into a state of aboulia. It wasn't a depression, although it had things in common with the depressive state I was already familiar with. So I took leave from the university where I taught. I went to Europe. Perhaps contact with beauty, with history, would jog me out of my state of numbness. I went to museums, visited ruins, and admired architectural monuments. In Paris, I watched the best films by French, German, and Italian filmmakers.

'But the trip only served to underline how out of touch with the world I was. Have you ever felt detached from your surroundings, Antonym? Because this was the feeling that had come over me. I came back from Europe with an urge to look for a solution in nature. Yes, I told myself, what I was missing was direct contact with reality in its rawest state. I needed something visceral. I spent two months visiting beautiful, remote places — beaches, forests, mountains, caves, waterfalls. But, no matter where I was, it was as if I wasn't there. There was a barrier between my conscious mind and my senses. I said "barrier", but perhaps "discontinuity" is more accurate. The noise of the rapids and waterfalls was dull when it reached my eardrums. I'd touch a leaf, and it would have no texture. I'd smell a flower, and its perfume would be a memory. I'd look at a green valley, and my gaze would go somewhere beyond, somewhere that didn't exist.

'It had always been like that, I now realised. I'd never been able to integrate with the world, surrender to the world. We operated on different frequencies — hence the feeling of discontinuity. One night, back in the city and more anaesthetised than ever, I came to the conclusion that the only way out of this state was through pain. So I stapled the fingers of my left hand, one by one. I did it several times. But not even my own screams could wake me. I understood something that might sound obvious to some: all pain, even the most tenuous, tends towards totality. It belongs to a parallel universe—there is no intersection between pain and reality, even though we believe the latter to be composed of painful elements. Pain, when it is attributed to the reality around us, as if it were something that made it even more real, is either a romantic metaphor or an ideological representation. When true pain sets in, we find we are removed from the world. This is one of the reasons why it is so terrible. Even the hardest, most burdensome life is better than pain. With no alternative, all I could do was try to forget myself. In a way, it's what everyone—OK, almost everyone—does.'

'What about sex?'

'My depression had left me impotent.'

'There are medications, in case one of your waiters hasn't already told you.'

'Which only work if you feel desire, and desire had been deleted from my brain's list of commands. Are you tired of listening to me?'

'No. At least not to the point of stapling the fingers of my left hand.'

'You should take me seriously. And you should take yourself seriously, Antonym. That's what I expect of you.'

'If it's what you expect of me … So you decided to forget yourself, and …?'

'I went back to my job at the university and wrote reviews for the literary supplement of a newspaper to top up my income. About three months went past, when this bleak routine took a detour. One Friday morning, I ran into an acquaintance as I was leaving the bank. My branch is in the shopping centre next door. He was coming out of an elegant jewellery store when we saw one another. We'd gone to school together and, though we'd come from different social echelons (he was very rich and I was very middle class), we'd become buddies. When we finished school, we'd followed the paths dictated by our vocations and bank accounts. I went on to study Language and Literature at the public university; he, Economics in London. And we'd never seen each other since.

'But when we met outside the bank he showed an enthusiasm that I can only describe as inexplicable. For my part, I pretended to be happy to see him after so many years, asking questions whose answers I wasn't even remotely interested in. My act was so convincing that he invited me to dinner that Saturday, in a restaurant that had recently opened. Since I was single, he wanted to introduce me to a friend of his wife's. The four of us could go out together; what did I think? At best, I didn't think anything. At worst, it was a fucking stupid idea. I fought the instinct to choose the path dictated by the second response. I accepted the invitation. Pleased I'd agreed, he gave me a hug (a rich man's hug, emanating a slight trace of musk), and added that it was about time we rekindled our friendship. I not only agreed, but I also lied and said I'd thought about trying to track him down recently. He said that we'd have plenty of opportunities to make up for lost time. I got his card; he jotted down my number. Our arrangements included a whisky at his place before dinner at the restaurant. When he got into his flashy car, surrounded by security guards, I sighed with regret. But there was no turning back. I had a date for the next day.

'At the agreed time, I arrived at my former classmate's home. The couple's friend was very attractive. She was about thirty-four, with a little body, tight from working out, and accentuated by a low-cut dress with slits up the sides.'

'Thirty-four …'

'What about it?'

'I love women about that age. They're still spring-like, but starting to show signs of the autumn to come.'

'Your images have been better.'

'I know. It's no accident I'm up shit creek.'

'Anyway, there was this gorgeous woman. She was friendly, and said she enjoyed reading my reviews and had bought the little book I'd written on twentieth-century Italian poetry (in which, incidentally, I used many of your observations, Antonym). Then she told me that she was married to a powerful senator, who was abroad at the time. Before we left for dinner, she and my friend's wife went to the bathroom to touch up their makeup—at least, that was their excuse. My friend took advantage of their absence to ask me straight up if I was interested in the senator's wife. I said I was. He told me that I should feel free to make a move. The senator wasn't too partial to sex, and his constant travels allowed his wife to have sexual escapades. He himself had already "served the nation", he revealed with a wink.

'When they came back from the bathroom, we had another dose of whisky, which had the effect of freeing the woman and me of any inhibition. Sitting in the back seat of the car, I ran my hand over her thighs, while she gently massaged my dormant penis. At the entrance to the restaurant, she patted my arse. My friend's wife must have seen this because she whispered something in his ear that made him chuckle. All very vulgar.

'In the restaurant, the petting continued under the table. I felt light, and so carefree that I hardly spoke during dinner. Since my thoughts were disposable anyway, I focused on the food being served. And focusing on one's food means to chew it slowly and to gently wet it with one's saliva in order to excite the most insignificant taste buds — all those things that are barely contained by the verb "to savour".

'Somewhere between the salad and the main course (a magnificent pasta sprinkled with white Piedmont truffles), behold, I began to see the world with a clarity I can only call supreme. How much time I had wasted, for God's sake! Everything was so close, so simple ... With each forkful, my clots of unhappiness dissolved and my blood flowed, expelling my torpor. I was being reborn from the mildew of my inflated self-image — and in my true size. My search ended there where my little "big truth" had begun — in the fleeting happiness that had washed over me during dinner. Through my palate, I had recovered my senses in a pure state. I was reliving the childhood of man, not as a regression, but as a triumph. I was about to embark on a new story: my own.'

'I know — it was the white Piedmont truffles.'

'Maybe one day you'll reach the dimension I'm talking about, Antonym.'

'It's just that I find it funny that you had an epiphany (can I call it that?) while dining with a slut.'

'It is this banality — or vulgarity, if you like — that makes this particular fact all the more relevant. It was at this moment that I decided to open my own restaurant; a restaurant different from all others. Actually, the word "restaurant", or "steakhouse", doesn't really express my intention to build a temple dedicated to satisfying the senses.'

'The blackmail ...'

'That evening, I recovered my potency with the senator's wife. We fucked four times that night, and to this day I get horny just remembering that shameless little whore's screams. The next day, my friend called me. From his insistence that I describe the most obscene details, I gathered he was a voyeur. I was right. He confessed his perversion, which was shared by his wife, and proposed that we secretly videotape me having sex with his wife's friend. The equipment would be installed in a flat that he'd lend me for our dates. I agreed.

'My friend, however, never got his hands on the tapes. I used them to blackmail the limp senator and his nymphomaniac wife. I also got a nice sum from my rich friend, who didn't want to be publicly known as a voyeur. When I got death threats from them, I told them that copies of the tapes, along with a letter in which I accused them of my murder, were in the hands of a friend who lived abroad. To be honest, the friend lives here. Anyway, to cut a long story short, I came out of it all with more than enough money to set up my own restaurant.'

'A temple in honour of anti-intellectualism, and built on sin.'

'My anti-intellectualism, Antonym, if it can be called that, is the fruit of one who used to entertain intellectual ambitions and then realised how much they can hold you back from life. Don't mistake it, please, for an apology for human idiocy. As for sin, well … That, too, is God's work.'

'How curious … Do you know Farfarello?'

'The priest? Of course I do.'

' "I will destroy the wisdom of the wise, and the intelligence of the intelligent I will reject. Where is the wise man? Where is the scholar?"'

'I have to admit that it was actually Farfarello's idea to put that biblical quote over the entrance. But I haven't seen him for a while.'

# VIII

Antonym hoped a good night's sleep would be enough to erase the feeling of delirium brought on by the dinner at Hemistich's restaurant. But it only made it grow. It hadn't been a dinner, but a ritual in which he'd unintentionally taken part. Why had Hemistich invited him? To persuade him to swell the ranks of his Christian hedonism? The expression 'Christian hedonism', an apparent paradox, had come into his mind because it had been the subject of an interview he'd done some two years earlier with a historian of religion who'd written a book about it. The only reason Antonym had been chosen to interview him was that he'd studied at a Catholic school. The result had been a mess but, luckily for Antonym, no one read the cultural section of the Sunday paper.

From what he could remember, this so-called 'Christian hedonism' was based on simple logic: if it is God's will that all men be happy, and it is natural that men want to satisfy Him, the most logical thing to do is to make the most of the sensorial experiences provided by the Creator. Could Hemistich, therefore, be defined as a Christian hedonist? Antonym decided he couldn't. This was because both the tenets and the consequences of hedonism, whether Greek or Christian, were moral—and there certainly wasn't any morality in Hemistich's deeds, discourse, or sensorial orgies.

In fact, the very idea that Hemistich had become religious struck him as absurd. He remembered that he only used to make reference to God, pretending to believe in Him, to impress those girls who made the sign of the Cross when they passed in front of a church. 'It's worth it; they're the hottest ones,' the sleaze used to say. As Antonym had already witnessed, Hemistich spoke about religion in a way that sounded highly original to the girls. Between one glass of wine and another, he borrowed from Pascal's Wager, using the sophism born of the seventeenth-century French philosopher's fertile imagination. While the lass he wanted to bed looked on questioningly, Hemistich would explain that, in order to rationally prove the existence of God, Blaise Pascal had argued that, from the point of view of mathematical probability, not to mention pragmatism and voluntarism, it didn't make sense to believe He didn't exist.

'The argument goes like this, my dear: if you believe God exists and it turns out to be true, you'll be rewarded with salvation, glory, eternal life and whatever else. If you believe God exists, but it turns out He doesn't, you don't lose anything for having believed. The opposite, however, offers no advantage: if you believe God doesn't exist and it turns out He does, all you have to look forward to is damnation and misery. If you believe God doesn't exist and He doesn't, you don't lose anything for having been a sceptic. It thus makes more sense to believe in God seeing that, in the best-case scenario, one has everything to gain and, in the worst, won't suffer because of it. To us, my gorgeous. Cheers.'

The girls who made the sign of the Cross when they

passed in front of a church were enchanted by Hemistich Pascal's words — and started to believe in the existence of his feelings when they had much more to gain by not believing.

No, Hemistich hadn't changed. He was the same bullshit artist as always, although he claimed the opposite. But what about his friendship with Farfarello? Perhaps 'friendship' was too strong a word. Nevertheless, the priest had suggested that Hemistich place the biblical quote over the restaurant door — and there was that line about God creating sin, which Hemistich had uttered as if it were an echo of something he'd heard with his own ears from Farfarello's mouth ... Everything suggested an intimacy that went beyond mere acquaintance. The priest's spiel about Hegel — the Idea, great men — didn't fit ... Or did it? Antonym had asked Hemistich how he knew Farfarello, but he'd avoided the question. 'I'm late for an appointment,' he'd said, quickly excusing himself. It was some coincidence that he'd run into Farfarello shortly before the dinner at the steakhouse. Coincidence ... Was it really a coincidence? Now, that would be really silly: believing in Destiny with a capital 'D.'

Antonym was confused.

# IX

'You forgot this.'

'Funny, I thought *The Brothers Karamazov* was yours. Our things got so mixed up over the last ten years that I ... Thanks.'

'I have to admit, I only finished reading it last week. I'd never managed to get past the first forty pages.'

'I always suspected you hadn't read everything you said you had. Journalists ...'

'Anyway, I don't mean to impose ...'

'Want a coffee?'

'OK.'

He followed Bernadette into the kitchen. She'd made a nest all her own, in which he recognised objects that were once part of the scenario of their life together.

'These things that used to be in our home and now are here ... They're like debris from a shipwreck washed up on a quiet beach.'

'That's what they are: debris from a shipwreck. You're still good at coming up with images. Aren't you going to write any more?'

'I'm helping a guy on an in-house newspaper.'

'Is that enough?'

'To get by, it is. From a financial point of view, I mean.'

'What about from other points of view?'

'I don't have other points of view any more. Even the financial one's hard enough to maintain.'

'You seem pretty depressed.'

'What did you expect?'

'That you'd get better after we broke up. When you were with me, you always seemed so unhappy.'

'You always wanted a big house with a garden and a dog … and this flat's so …'

'So small. But who said I've given up my dreams? This is just my launch pad.'

'You never were good at images. Are you still at the bureau?'

'I am, but I'm getting ready to open my own office. I've rented a place with a partner.'

'A partner. Right. What's his name?'

'It doesn't matter. You don't know him.'

'Let's see if I don't know him … Is he …?'

'Coffee's ready.'

'You cheated on me.'

'Antonym, please don't make things any more difficult.'

'You cheated.'

'It's a woman, Antonym.'

'What's her name?'

'…'

'It's a guy. You're a terrible liar.'

'Get a detective to follow me. Aren't you going to drink your coffee?'

'I've got plans, too, you know.'

'Great.'

'Hemistich wants me to go into business with him.'

'To be a partner in that restaurant of his?'

'I'm not exactly sure. To be honest, he only said he wants me to work with him. We're going to discuss it a little further down the track.'

'I went to Hemistich's restaurant a while back. I didn't think it was anything special.'

'That's because you didn't go to what he calls a "closed-door event".'

'What's a closed-door event?'

'A special dinner he throws once a week. I'm always invited.'

'Is the food any different?'

'The food, the drinks, the people; everything is different from normal. These events are a real epiphany. I'm completely hooked now. When I'm there I have really intense, incredible feelings. I think I even have visions.'

'Visions? And here I was, thinking you'd stop at paranoia … You thought I wanted to kill you, remember? By pouring lead into your ear while you were asleep.'

'That was just a fantasy, Bernadette, which I never should have mentioned. But these visions … Those paintings of fauns and nymphs that come to life and skip down from the walls.'

'I didn't see any paintings of fauns or nymphs on the walls.'

'That decor's only used for special events; it's the same with the bullfights in the bar and the biblical quote at the door. Hemistich has spent a fortune installing moveable panels and walls and other contraptions. Curious, isn't it?'

'Indeed. It sounds like the normal restaurant's just a façade for these events.'

'Doesn't it?'

'...'

'...'

'Your coffee's waiting. One-and-a-half spoonfuls of sugar — is that still right?'

'Yes. Bernadette, do you … No, forget it …'

'What?'

'Bernadette, you believe in God. Do you think Evil is an integral part of His nature?'

'What?'

'Just answer …'

'It's strange you should ask me that.'

'Why?'

'You, who's always said religion should be classed as fantasy fiction.'

'That's actually an adaptation. Someone once said that metaphysics should be considered fantasy fiction.'

'Have you become religious?'

'Let's just say I'm tinkering with the subject. Come on, answer my question.'

'Isn't it God's will that even the innocent — including children — suffer in order to fulfil his plan?'

'Ivan Karamazov.'

'Yes. That's about as far as I can get.'

'Some scholars say Dostoyevsky meant that God exists because evil and pain exist. If the world were good, in essence, God wouldn't be necessary. From this point of view, therefore, I think one can say that Evil is an integral part not only of the divine plan, but also of His nature; God's nature.'

'You needn't have asked me anything.'

'The day I was fired from the paper, I remembered something you used to say: "It's impossible to love thy neighbour from up close," and so on. That's also Karamazov's.'

'I know. That's about as far as I can get.'

'I should have read more Dostoyevsky. There's no method to my reading. I've got so many gaps because of it. Russian literature, German philosophy … I've wasted time reading a heap of useless Italian literature.'

'To seduce mummy. *Mamma* Roma.'

'Mum … Living with her was unbearable, but sometimes I miss her so much. As for Dad, I don't know what to think …'

'I was really fond of her, too …'

'I know. And I'm jealous that you had your own relationship with my mother.'

'*Vitellone* …'

'Isn't it funny how there's still so much intimacy between us?'

'Intimacy takes a while to die, but one day it does.'

'Do you ever think about me?'

'I do, and I quickly stop. The last few years of our marriage were really hard going.'

'But we're friends, aren't we?'

'They still haven't invented a category for the current stage of our relationship. I have friendly feelings for you, but we're not friends. I miss you, but I don't want to be with you. I remember our past, but I'd like to forget it. Maybe, with time, we'll manage to become just ex-wife and ex-husband—the first step towards a mutual friendship—unless there's some kind of major conflict along the way. Anyway, it'd be worse if we'd had a kid.'

'You really wanted children …'

'I still do. You never did. You've always hated kids.'

'I don't hate kids. I just don't want any competition. I was thinking, we could go on a photography safari in Kenya. It's always been your dream. I know your dreams better than anyone does.'

'Antonym, I didn't want to tell you now, but you'd find out anyway, so it's better you hear it from me.'

'What?'

'I'm pregnant.'

'…'

'Are you OK?'

'No, I'm not.'

'You look pale. I'll get you a glass of water.'

'I was right. You cheated on me.'

'That's crazy. We broke up almost ten months ago, and I'm only two months pregnant.'

'I know you, Bernadette. You wouldn't get pregnant to a man you'd only just met. Who's this guy you've obviously been screwing for years—your partner?'

'No, he's not my partner and I haven't been screwing him for years. The guy, as you say, is an ex-boyfriend from when I was a teenager. I ran into him again at a resort.'

'At a resort! So, you hang around resorts now?'

'Would it make any difference to you if it had been … um, at the New York Plaza? I needed to unwind, and a friend

THE DAY I KILLED MY FATHER

suggested a resort. He also needed to get away from it all. He'd broken up with his wife a few months earlier ...'

'What a cock-and-bull story.'

'To sum up the cock-and-bull story, there was an amazing dinner he'd arranged to have served at his bungalow: a dazzling full moon on the veranda, divine wine, and a really big, soft, nice-smelling bed.'

'Spare me the sordid details. You forgot to mention the opportunistic bastard and the needy, irresponsible woman. What if he's got AIDS?'

'Don't be ridiculous, Antonym. But if it makes you feel any better, I haven't seen him since. He lives in another city. We spoke two or three times after that, always by phone, and that was it. The last time we spoke he told me he'd got back together with his wife.'

'And you bawled your eyes out, obviously, feeling used and abandoned. What's the bastard's name?'

'I can't say I was happy about it, but it didn't bother me that much either. To be honest, it helped reinforce my decision not to tell him anything.'

'He should pay for the abortion. You're going to have an abortion, of course. I'll pay.'

'I'm not having an abortion.'

'What do you mean?'

'I want a kid now. I'm already thirty-five, and finding a man who would meet my long list of requirements would take too much time. Not to mention the fact that the odds of my search failing are greater than my odds of success.'

'You've lost it ...'

'...'

'I'd like this kid to be mine, Bernadette. Why don't you have an abortion so we can have a baby of our own?'

'This conversation ends here, Antonym. When you get your head screwed on right, we can talk again.'

'You shouldn't have done this to me. I need you, and now a foetus has come between us. You're going to love this kid more than you ever loved me.'

'You need help, Antonym.'

'Not that psychologist crap again. You're the one who's sick, Bernadette. Who ever heard of having a kid like this?'

'You know what, Antonym? Go fuck yourself. Since we split up, I've been making plans that have a chance of working out. I no longer suffer from paralysis—your paralysis. Your inaction, your boredom, your depression contaminated me for a decade. A decade! It's what my analyst calls my "lost decade". The best thing that's happened in my life was breaking up with the sick person you've become. Your cynicism is the fruit of your frustration, your limitations—as a man, as a professional, as a human being. You're cynical, Antonym, because you're mediocre. And your cynicism is a comfortable way to hide this fact of life. I might not be anything special, Antonym, I might not know what I am, but I do know what I'm not. And I'm not like you, OK? Or, better, I'm not you. I'm me. Me.'

'Bernadette, I know this isn't the time for philosophy, but don't you see that the "self" is largely a construction based on an "other"? That the self doesn't exist entirely on its own, but is also built around an external gaze? Since I have been and am part of your existence, my self is a part of your self—and that's something you'll never be free of. It can't be taken back. This is everyone's hell.'

'Who do you think you are—some kind of Sartre? You want philosophy? Well, listen up: my self, which may actually contain a part of your self, no longer wants to see itself reflected in this other that is you. By bringing me down to your level, you tried to stop me from having the simplest, most precious, things in the world, Antonym. Where's the noise of children scampering through the house? Where are the family lunches on Sundays? Where are the holidays on the beach? Where's that comfortable boredom that people who love one another feel after years of life in common? Where are the plans: for a bigger house, an exotic holiday, a place in the country, for ... for ... For God's sake, Antonym, I don't despise everything middle class! I want to be middle-class, OK? I want to have noisy reactions like this. Do you hear me? Do you want that translated into psychologist crap? Well, here: I've smashed the mirror, Mr Narcissus, and in this other self, growing here in my womb, there won't be any of your self. None at all.'

'You're wrong, Bernadette! What hurts me most is knowing that my self—which shaped part of your self—will inhabit the self of the child of this guy who slept with you.'

'No, Antonym, this is all just another one of your abstractions. What hurts you most is the fact that I've got myself a life and fucked another guy. And enjoyed it! A blind man could tell you what you're feeling. It's called jealousy. And middle-class jealousy at that. Your story is pretty cock and bull, too, darling. Now get out.'

'Bernadette, I ...'

'I said, get out. I can't stand looking at you any more.'

'Can I take the book?'

'By all means. You're going to end up like Ivan Karamazov.'

# X

'You look upset. Wasn't it any good?'

'Of course it was … It's just that I had an argument with my ex that I can't get out of my head. She's pregnant to a guy she doesn't know, and she's going to keep it.'

'These ex-wives have always been a headache for me.'

'…'

'It's almost like a dream being here with you, you know.'

'A nightmare, you mean.'

'Oh, don't be so bitter, darling. If Jonah knew, he wouldn't believe it …'

'Who's Jonah, your whale?'

'Dickhead … A really intelligent guy I went out with years ago. We got along really well. But one day he said he needed to take some time out, travel around Europe. The last night … Wow, it was wild!'

'Then, bye-bye, Jonah?'

'Yeah. When the Berlin Wall came down, he'd just arrived in Germany. He even sent me a little piece of the wall. Cool, don't you think? He wrote a note saying that, unlike socialism, I wasn't one of his lost illusions. The guy was so fucking creative.'

'So why wouldn't lost-illusions Jonah believe we're fucking?'

'Oh, don't talk like that—"fucking." We're having a relationship.'

'OK, so why wouldn't lost-illusions Jonah believe we're relating by fucking?'

'You're a lost cause, you know … Because Jonah also really liked your journalism.'

'So one of my twenty-five readers was a backpacking communist.'

'There was this news item once about a banker who spent much more on the guard dogs at his branches than his employees. Then you wrote in the paper that that was an apt illustration of the difference between socialists and social democrats: while the socialists wanted the bank employees to earn more than the dogs, the social democrats would be happy if they made the same. Jonah laughed his head off and used to tell it to everyone.'

'I didn't write that.'

'Yes, you did.'

'What an idiot I was.'

'Jeez, you're in a bad mood.'

'I've had it with journalism, but I need to think about what I'm going to do for a living. My job on that in-house paper finishes next month. Hemistich said he was going to make me a proposal … Have you heard anything about that, Kiki?'

'No. He'd kill me if he knew we've been together so many months. Actually, you swore you wouldn't say anything.'

'I won't say anything. But I don't get why you're so scared of him. You're free, I'm free …'

'I'm not that free. How do you think I pay my bills?'

'By renting out the properties you inherited. That's what you told me.'

'I lied.'

'You lied?'

'I lied. I don't have any properties, and I live in a rented flat. To be honest, I live on what Hemistich pays me.'

'You're paid by Hemistich? What does he pay you to do?'

'To help with what he calls "persuasion tactics".'

'Which is …'

'Having sex with the guys he wants to draw into what he calls his "sphere of influence". I'm like a continuation of the special events.'

'You're a whore.'

'No need to be insulting.'

'Does he pay you to go out with me?'

'He paid for me to go out with you in the first two months. Then he said it wasn't necessary any more and that I should step away because "the work was done".'

'So why do you keep having it off with me?'

'Don't you see? I'm in love with you.'

'But I'm not such a good fuck.'

'I think you're great. You know, when we saw each other in the restaurant the first time, I could tell something was going to happen between us. You gave me a special look.'

'I was looking at your arse.'

'Pig.'

'…'

'Do you love me?'

'No.'

'I'm leaving.'

'Don't be such a baby, Kiki. I like you a lot. For me, it's practically the same thing.'

'Why do you like me?'

'Because you're special.'

'I like the sound of that. Why am I special?'

'Women are all the same in their flaws, and different in their qualities.'

'Well …?'

'Well, what?'

'What are the qualities that make me different from other women?'

'These here …'

'Ah, you're tickling me, you clown.'

'Kiki, what do you know about Hemistich's events that I don't?'

'I'm sick of talking about that. Let's make love again.'

'Either you tell me or we're finished.'

'Do you think Hemistich tells me anything? I know what everyone else involved knows: once a week, he transforms the restaurant into what you saw, and it becomes the venue for an orgy.'

'That's all?'

'That's all … Well, come to think of it, there has been the odd event outside the restaurant.'

'Outside the restaurant, where?'

'In this huge country house about forty minutes out of town.'

'Hemistich never told me there were events in a country house.'

'You should've seen them! They'd go on for two whole days; total madness. I'd come back a wreck. The upside is that I got paid double to participate.'

'Do you know when the next one is?'

'No, I don't. I think they've been on hold ever since Augusto died.'

'The Augusto that killed his wife and committed suicide?'

'Yeah.'

'Did you know him?'

'Of course I did. But don't worry. He wasn't as good as you, darling.'

'You're so irritating! I'm not worried about that, you idiot.'

'Me, an idiot? I'm not telling you anything else. You've hurt my feelings.'

'I'm sorry, Kiki, it's just that I really want to know more about Augusto. We were friends for a while.'

'OK, I forgive you. Augusto participated in Hemistich's events.'

'Right, so Augusto commits this incredible act of violence, and there hasn't been an event outside the restaurant since. What's the connection?'

'And I'm supposed to be the idiot! Augusto did what he did at one of these events.'

'I'm shocked. Hemistich didn't tell me any of this.'

'Do you think he'd go around blabbing about it?'

'Did you see them die?'

'I'm not saying anything else.'

'Do you or don't you want to keep seeing me?'

'Promise you won't tell anyone?'

'I promise.'

'Do you swear on your mother's life?'

'My mother's dead.'

'Swear on your dad's life.'

'He's not worth it.'

'Then swear on your mother's grave.'

'I swear, I swear. What a drag, Kiki …'

'I didn't see them die … It's hard for me to talk about these things.'

'Make an effort.'

'Augusto used to show up alone, but that night he brought his wife. I remember she was really impressed by the décor of the house. The candles everywhere, the same figures as in the restaurant on the walls … Satyrs and nymphs — that's what they're called, isn't it? I've never been good at mythology.'

'So what do you think you saw?'

'Well, when things had really heated up — people fucking, left, right, and centre — I decided to play a game with two hot guys who were dying to do me. I told them that if they really wanted me they'd have to catch me. I took off running, and they came after me. We ended up heading away from the halls and down a winding corridor that went underground. This corridor seemed to go on forever, and other corridors ran off it as if it were all part of a labyrinth. I think it was a labyrinth. Because I was really wasted (Hemistich's wine must be laced with some kind of drug), it took me a while to realise the guys weren't behind me any more. When it dawned on me that I was alone, I was scared — especially because, by that time, there was no light. I froze, panting, for several minutes. I was dizzy, freaked out, and really needed to go to the toilet.

After taking several deep breaths, I started to head back. I went slowly, because each step took so much energy. I was in a really bad way, and lost. I'd gone about thirty metres, when I heard a horrible scream. My heart started racing faster than ever, and I felt as if I was about to faint. I tried to cry for help, but my voice stuck in my throat, like in a nightmare. I was scared stiff, but this time I didn't freeze. It was the fainting feeling that pushed me forward—if I was going to faint, I wanted to be in the light, and with other people. Feeling my way along the walls, I went a little further, until I noticed a sliver of light at ground level at the end of one of the corridors. *It's coming from under a door. It might be a shortcut back to the halls*, I thought. So I headed for the door. Behind it, two men were talking. I pressed my ear to the door and … Oh, that's enough. I'm going to get myself into trouble.'

'You pressed your ear to the door and …'

'One of the voices was Hemistich's.'

'What was he saying?'

' "It's over." I wanted to open the door to get out of that dark corridor, but those words made me hesitate. I don't know why, but I imagined that the scream I'd heard had come from there.'

'Well, had it?'

'I think so. What do you think?'

'How am I supposed to know? What did you do next?'

'I got out of there as fast as possible, because I was afraid they'd see me. I found my way back quickly, thank God.'

'What Hemistich said, was that the only thing you heard?'

'No, I also heard the other man's answer.'

'Let's have it, Kiki.'

' "Nothing's over. This is just the beginning for us." '

'That's it?'

'Yes.'

'Did you recognise the voice?'

'I recognised it an hour later, when Hemistich interrupted the event to say Augusto had killed his wife and committed suicide.'

'The voice belonged to one of the guests.'

'No, it was the priest who Hemistich had just called.'

'Farfarello.'

'Farfarello, that's it. How do you know?'

'Let's see if I've got this right: Hemistich told everyone he'd just called Farfarello, but you say you heard his voice an hour earlier.'

'That's right.'

'And what did Hemistich say to justify Farfarello's presence?'

'He said he'd called the priest to provide spiritual assistance.'

'For the dead.'

'For the dead.'

'Spiritual assistance for the dead. Didn't anyone find this nonsense suspicious?'

'It's not nonsense. He prayed for the salvation of Augusto and his wife. It was quite touching.'

'Kiki, can't you see that Farfarello probably helped

Hemistich kill them?'

'They wouldn't kill anyone, Antonym. The police conducted a thorough investigation. They took statements from everyone, examined the crime scene, and concluded that it was a homicide followed by a suicide.'

'And was the crime scene the room behind that door?'

'Everything seems to point to it.'

'Did the police take a statement from Farfarello?'

'No, because he wasn't one of the guests. He wasn't there when it all happened. I mean ...'

'You mean in spite of all their care, it was possible to trick the police.'

'I didn't trick anyone. The detective didn't ask me anything about a priest.'

'Did he ask you where you were at the time of the deaths?'

'He did, and I told him I was in the wood next to the house with the guys who'd chased me—which they confirmed without me even asking. I didn't want any hassles. Not with the police, or Hemistich.'

'So you lied to the police.'

'I lied a little, so what?'

'So, just as you lied to the police, you might be lying to me.'

'Where are you going with this?'

'How do I know you didn't take part in the crime?'

'You're crazy!'

'How do I know you didn't see the crime?'

'I swear I didn't see it, and I didn't do anything. I've told you the whole truth. And now you have to swear again that

you won't tell anyone anything. Do you swear?'
   'I've already sworn.'
   'Swear again.'

# XI

It was already dawn when Antonym parked his car near the beach he used to go to when he was first married. He walked a hundred metres along a narrow path down to the sand. Perfume from the flowers leaning over the walls of the houses was gradually replaced with the smell of the sea air that hinted at the infinite horizon. Gazing at the sea as it recovered its blue hues in the morning light, Antonym was hoping to recover something as well—something of his own essence. But it wasn't long before this hope evaporated. For a few minutes he watched the birth and death of the waves, noticing those that interrupted their brief existence on the rocks, and scrutinised the hills framing the small bay. Nothing. Then a poem that Eugenio Montale had dedicated to the Mediterranean came into his head:

> *Antico, sono ubriacato dalla voce*
> *che esce dalle tue bocche quando si schiudono*
> *come verdi campane e si ributtano*
> *indietro e si disciolgono.*
> *La casa delle mie estati lontane*
> *t'era accanto, lo sai,*
> *là nel paese dove il sole cuoce*
> *e annuvolano l'aria le zanzare.*

*Come allora oggi in tua presenza impietro,*
*mare, ma non più degno*
*mi credo del solenne ammonimento*
*del tuo respiro. Tu m'hai detto primo*
*che il piccino fermento*
*del mio cuore non era che un momento*
*del tuo; che mi era in fondo*
*la tua legge rischiosa: esser vasto e diverso*
*e insieme fisso:*
*e svuotarmi così d'ogni lordura*
*come tu fai che sbatti sulle sponde*
*tra sugheri alghe asterie*
*le inutili macerie del tuo abisso.*[†]

Antònym recited the poem to himself. Ten years before, it had moved him. Now, it was like repeating a shopping list. Montale was still grand, but he, Antonym, had lost his connection with poetry. Perhaps because poetry, deep down,

---

† I'm drunk with that voice, archaic sea / pouring from your mouths when they gape / like green bells and are shocked / back and dissolved. / The house of my distant summers, / as you know, belonged to you / there in that country of scorching suns / and low air fogged with midges. / Stunned now, as I once was, in your presence / I no longer believe myself worth / the solemn exhortation of your breath. / It was you who first taught me / my heart's puny tumult / was only a moment of yours —/ that at bottom I kept your hazardous / law: to be vast and various / yet steady: / and so to purge myself of rubbish / as you do, hurling on the beaches / among starfish corks seaweed / the waste of your abyss. ('Antico', English translation by Sonia Raiziss and Alfredo de Palchi, *Selected Poems*, New Directions, 1975.)

is a highly personal experience, of which one can only grasp the surface at best. And this surface ended up losing its meaning, like a postcard landscape admired to exhaustion. Antonym stared at the sea, but didn't see anything beyond the vulgar beauty that so charmed tourists. A wry smile spread across his face; attributing transcendence to it all seemed pathetically trite. Maybe Montale was just an idiot, trying to give meaning to that which had none. Maybe there was no depth whatsoever in poetry and it was just surface.

Now he was numb. '*Il mare è di tutti quelli che lo stanno ad ascoltare,*' '*Il mare è di ...*' *Who'd said that? The Sicilian writer Giovanni Verga, perhaps ... Yes, it was Verga.* Why he had once read Verga he could no longer fathom. Verga's Aci Trezza, where Ulysses had visited, seemed so far away ... Now Ulysses was a man with somewhere to return to. The world is less threatening when you have somewhere to return to, or was it the opposite? And this question ... How many useless questions do we ask ourselves in the course of a lifetime? Was this a measure of our own utter insignificance? Maybe he should staple his fingers, as Hemistich had done, to at least feel pain—in the hope that waiting for the pain to cease would give meaning, even if only ephemeral, to some minuscule fleck of his existence. The meaning of life: how many jokes had been made about such nonsense? But was it really nonsense? Maybe he should have a child (Bernadette was having one, wasn't she?) to resuscitate some kind of emotion. But what woman would want to bear his child? Antonym laughed again. A child ... Not even with Bernadette. He'd been lying when he proposed they have one, and deep down Bernadette knew it. A child who was a failure or who outshone him—either outcome would be unbearable.

Maybe, maybe, maybe. Maybe he should kill himself, as Augusto had done. It wasn't the first time he'd considered suicide, but the truth was that he'd never felt his existence was tragic enough to take this path of no return. Not even now, come to think of it. One had to take oneself really seriously, which he was incapable of doing—although, granted, he didn't like the idea of being supplanted or disappointed by a child. Even in his moments of desperation, he often allowed himself to drift into banal thoughts. Was he less human because of it? Or more human? After all, wasn't being human contenting oneself with surface? There was surface again. The problem was that he was unable to be entirely superficial or entirely profound. Augusto hadn't struck him as terribly profound either, although he had left that poem. But if poetry is surface …

Augusto … He kept brooding over the story that Kiki had told him the night before, but it was impossible to know for sure in what way Hemistich and Farfarello had been involved in it. Might they have helped Augusto murder his wife, and then killed him? Had they been Augusto's accomplices, and then watched him commit suicide? Did they simply witness the deaths, without interfering? Even in this last case, they wouldn't be free of guilt; they'd be accessories. The only way to find out would be to ask Hemistich, but Antonym was less afraid of the answer than of the consequences of doing this. No matter what the answer, it would connect him to the fact and, by extension, to Hemistich.

Antonym gazed at a tree trunk, dirty with tar, that had

been carried onto the sand by the sea. *'Le inutili macerie del tuo abisso …'* He was seized by the idea that he himself was good for nothing—just excrement in an ocean of other worthless existences. What had he done with his life to this point? Nothing. He hadn't been able to love those who loved him (and there had been so few!), and he hadn't produced anything of relevance in anything he'd turned his hand to (except in the opinion of Kiki and her backpacking ex-boyfriend—but Kiki and her crowd were a load of rubbish, too). What kind of epitaph would excrement like he have? Gazing at the seascape—which was, in itself, an invitation to live—he tried to come up with a phrase that, on his death, would sum up his idiotic existence. And at that moment he fancied he heard a voice, mingling with the sea breeze, whispering in his ear: *Here lies he who died without ever having been.*

Died without ever having been. But having been what? And then a light came on in Antonym's mind. *Without ever having been a man of spirit.* Yes, that was what he wanted to be: a man who, through personal enterprise, would help change the fate of the world. This ambition was what was stopping him from being 'a normal man', as Bernadette liked to say. The fact that he hadn't fulfilled it had often led him to feel dead or that he could be approaching death—perhaps even at the hand of Bernadette, who wanted him to be 'normal'. Ever since he'd been a child, Antonym had felt different, special, but without ever lighting upon what it was that made him special. All those moments of anxiety that had punctuated his life, all those empty afternoons munching on biscuits, all those idiotic articles. They were symptoms not of his vacuity, as he had always thought, but of anticipation.

Antonym took a deep breath, his eyes closed. *'Ubriacato dalla voce che esce dalle tue bocche quando si schiudono come verdi campane e si ributtano indietro e si disciolgono.'* No, poetry wasn't just surface—not to one who decided to make his own life poetry. Yes, that was what he had to do: give his existence a poetic dimension. Brutally poetic. All great men had done this somehow—the good ones and the bad ones. But what is Good and what is Evil? If God couldn't exist without Evil, if Evil was also a part of the divine plan, then ... Then, that was it! One couldn't judge men of spirit, because all of them were fulfilling God's designs. What did it matter if, in the lines they composed, a few worthless little lives were lost along the way? It was the big picture that mattered. The big picture!

He could no longer condemn Hemistich and Farfarello. They were obviously partners in an undertaking with a higher objective. Yes, that was it: a new religion! A religion that celebrated the senses as the only way to understand the world ... Life and Death ... Augusto. Hemistich had said that Augusto had acted on his own impulse: 'The purest expression of the senses.' No, there was no flippancy in this remark. Hemistich and Farfarello had witnessed the deaths of Augusto and his wife. No one was that flippant. Perhaps they were true men of spirit, the founders of a new way. A way that contained a dash of Evil, certainly. But, since Evil was a part of the divine design, there always had to be someone to do the dirty work. And if this fate—doing the dirty work essential to the divine plan—was born of human free will, he who stepped forward to play the part had to be considered by God to be a special child. A child who loved Him so much he was willing to relinquish the advantages of Good; who was willing to face limbo, hell, or whatever else, so that God could bask in glory. Evil was thus a parallel highway to the highway of Good—and both met in infinity. The infinity that was God!

A religion of the senses that led to total knowledge. Was he, Antonym, prepared to be an apostle? Obviously, this was what Hemistich was going to propose to him. He and Farfarello had drawn him in because they had sensed the potential in him. They regarded him as a man of spirit, which in some ways he had always felt himself to be, though he had never admitted it to himself until then. No, he wouldn't die without ever having been. No, he …

What nonsense to imagine he was any different to that tree trunk smeared with tar that the sea had deposited on the sand! How naive, how presumptuous!

Antonym watched a solitary seagull flying in imperfect circles over the ocean. He was also alone, also flying in imperfect circles. But soon his face lit up. Presumption and naivety: weren't these also the attributes of a man of spirit? Many great men had been ridiculed early on in their careers for seeming overly ambitious and out of touch with reality. What if 'realistic' was just a euphemism for the weak, for those devoid of spirit?

Antonym realised, then, which God he had begun to believe in since his life had entered this jumble of events and thoughts. It was the God who had given him, Antonym, the capacity to stand out from the flock. It was the God who had taken him far beyond Good and Evil. It was the Entity who had created the Universe—the genesis of all presumption and all naivety—and had thus become God. *I will destroy the wisdom of the wise, and the intelligence of the intelligent I will reject. Where is the wise man? Where is the scholar?'* Now he understood the real meaning of those words.

And this was how God appeared to Antonym, and Antonym appeared as God before God. Terrible events were to follow henceforth.

# Part Two

–12–

I was hoping you'd say something immediately after the last reading session, but you left without saying a thing. I take it you didn't like it ... I can understand what you mean when you say it's a disturbing book. I stopped writing it shortly before I killed my father, when I was swept up in the events that led me to commit patricide. What ... ? That's not true. I wasn't emulating my characters when I eliminated my father ... I'm sorry, but that kind of comment is uncalled for ... No, I don't want to hear it ... What? What idiotic manual gave you the idea that using the word 'eliminate' is typical of those who premeditate murder in cold blood? I give you the most precious thing I have, and this is how you reward me. More than an attempt at writing literature, my unfinished book is a concrete representation of my interrupted life, and this is why it is of inestimable value to me. It's confirmation that I've managed to become the protagonist of my own story. I decided to kill my father, I decided to stop writing my book, I decided ...

No, it's not true that it might have been my only option. I could have gone on living as if nothing had happened. But in choosing the path I did, I put a full stop to everything. Do you see? I imposed my will on everyone. Even you, who had nothing to do with this whole story, but who is now living and breathing it and will remember it until the day you die … Yes, I did kill my father, as one breathes—but that illustrates how resolute I was in my decision rather than the lack of an alternative. It was a conscious move—lucid, rational even; the adjective doesn't matter. I couldn't care less that people think I'm crazy, or that I'm here, in this place, because doctors and judges have declared me insane. I'm not crazy, do you hear me? I'm not crazy.

Isn't it clear to you why I killed my father? Then I have no illumination to offer. Only darkness.

I had dearly hoped for an unbiased appreciation of my book, and now you come along with these … You've cheapened me, and what I wrote, by drawing easy, mechanical parallels. I didn't expect such stupidity from you. Please, leave, and never come back.

## 13

It's been ten days since we last saw each other—long enough for me to calm down and come to the conclusion that I owe you an apology. Can you forgive me?

You see, I was fantasising about seducing you with my book. After all, that's what books are really for—to seduce. But you, it seems, were not seduced. You wanted to read meanings into it that ... Come on, say it. Why do you think I emulated my characters? In other words, that the book anticipates my patricide? You think 'anticipates' is too strong a term? Then use another. 'Is connected to', perhaps.

*The Brothers Karamazov* is the story of a patricide. So what? The fact that I mention it doesn't mean I intended to kill my father; it's just that it deals with some of my philosophical and religious concerns—because it debates the existence of God ... Coincidence? Yes. Can you allow me the right to coincidences, or is that asking too much?

How curious ... Did I tell you this at the beginning of our conversation? That after killing my father as one breathes, I leaned the piece of wood against the back of the couch, as if it were a ritualistic object? I'd forgotten that detail. It's true ... for Hemistich and Farfarello, Augusto's death also had something ritualistic about it. Yes, Antonym would have turned out like them. Do you know what else? Contrary to what I first thought, I now believe that you were seduced by my book—even more than I'd hoped. I bet you haven't thought about anything else this whole time. I, at least, have only thought about you.

I apologise again. I didn't mean to make you uncomfortable. Don't get me wrong—it's just that you've become my only connection with … I don't know what. I was going to say 'the outside world', but that's not true. You don't bring in anything from the outside. Our only topic is me, my history, what I did. But, in a way, you are the outside world—a piece of it. You're another voice, at least. I haven't heard another voice for days, not even my own. It's my isolation. I don't have anyone else—just you. And I'll lose you when our conversation is over. You'll never come back, I know … Don't make a promise you can't keep. I hate it when people feel sorry for me. I'm a murderer, a parricide. I don't deserve pity, nor do I want it.

Reading the book—your reading of the book, that is—has unsettled me. You read it with so much interest. I'm no longer sure if I'm happy it's not finished. Your vivid interest—I could tell from the way you read it—planted a seed of doubt in my mind. And I don't need this uncertainty, do you hear, because not even a parricide deserves to be tortured like this … What uncertainty? That maybe I had no other option. No, I can't think about it. I need to breathe a little, I need to breathe … The dizziness, oh dear, the dizziness is back …

## 14

I'm fine, thank you. No, the dizziness didn't come back; it was all in my mind. We can talk. Don't worry, I'm back under control. My uncertainty has gone, and everything is clear again.

Let's get straight to the point. I told you that reading my book would help you understand some of my processes. Some. And these processes are intellectual ... Go ahead ... Antonym says at one stage that his father isn't worth it. So what? It's a line — laden with self-reference, I admit — that only reinforces my intention to distance myself, through writing the book, from the real relationship that consumed me.

Don't look for clues in the plot itself, please. That's vulgar. What I have to say is of much more interest to you. And it will make everything clearer. You want clarity, don't you?

I wanted, as I've said before, to speculate about the birth of Evil, after I'd acquired some knowledge of philosophy, literature, and existential matters ... What? I don't mean to offend you, but that's a narrow view of the matter. Try to be less of an analyst and more of a philosopher. It is true that science explains that we are born with genetic determinants which can be developed or stifled by our environment. It is also true that psychology can provide explanations for my blasphemies when I was a boy, and much of what followed. But that's not my point. It's more transcendental than that. I was interested, I repeat, in finding out what lies beyond our genes, and their psychological or social triggers.

Let's take a historical case: Hitler. Some people believe that his artistic frustrations and repressed homosexuality led him to do all those horrific deeds, as if they had activated hypothetical genes for Evil. But if they were the only factors, there would have been hundreds of monsters of Hitler's calibre throughout human history—and there haven't been. Hitler's followers? They only confirm my theory. They were so petty that they would have been insignificant, or would only have been common criminals, were it not for Hitler. Now, consider the opposite: Good. Take the example of Saint Francis of Assisi. In an era of utter moral and religious decay, he renounced wealth to assume a life dedicated to Christ and the poor. He attracted thousands of followers, but there is no record of any of them having attained the same degree of sainthood and abnegation. Can hypothetical genes for Good explain Saint Francis? If that were the case, shouldn't there be lots of others like him?

Where am I going with this? Well, you read *Future*. I'm suggesting that there are men of spirit, good ones and evil ones, who are granted complete free will. It is men of spirit who drive humanity and, one way or another, who fulfil God's designs ... How can divine designs and free will coexist? That's the point I'd like to have elaborated on in my book: God's designs are universal, but they are brought to fruition by the free will of special individuals. In other words, there had to be a Saint Francis, just as it was imperative that there be a Hitler, so that humanity could follow the path laid out by God. But Saint Francis only became Saint Francis, and Hitler only became Hitler, because they were given the ability to choose. The former chose Good; the latter, Evil. Which also means that Saint Francis could have chosen Evil, and Hitler, Good … Yes, in a way, they were equal at some stage. That's another heresy for my list.

You're right; most people choose their own path. But, unless they're men of spirit, their power is undeniably limited by inner forces, by the instinct to follow the herd. For them, their will isn't as free as they think it is. That's what allows God to forgive the sins of the small … I beg your pardon? Can a monster like Hitler be forgiven? Well, based on the assumption that his entirely free choice is a part of the divine plan, I believe so. As it says in the last chapter of *Future*, Good and Evil are parallels that meet at the infinity that is God. But perhaps the idea of forgiving men of spirit who choose Evil is beyond human understanding.

My ability to converse with literary and philosophical traditions? You'd make a great literary critic, you know. You've perfected the art of saying nothing while creating the impression that you're saying everything. The sarcasm again — forgive me. Remember the passage where I write that Antonym, to pass the time, liked to make free associations? Well, his favourite association is actually a line from a *commedia dell'arte* character, Il Dottore. That's what dialoguing is: stealing.

What would have become of Antonym? He believed himself to be a man of spirit, but he wasn't really. If I'd continued the book, Antonym would have formed a trinity with Hemistich and Farfarello. His baptism into the darkness of the religion of the senses would have been to kill Kiki, in a ritual similar to the one in which Augusto killed his wife. The aboulic, mistrustful Antonym would transform into an eloquent preacher, with an enormous talent for drawing people with money to the new religion. The enthusiasm of neophytes, you know.

Thanks to Antonym, the orgies would become more and more fantastic, and the evil ones would build a kind of cathedral of pleasure, far from the city. The success of the undertaking would attract the greed of extortionists connected to the police, and of those who dealt in the hallucinogenic weed that animated the parties. The situation would get complicated. To stop the business from crumbling, Farfarello would suggest to Antonym that, without Hemistich's knowledge, he should approach the senator he had blackmailed in the first place. Using his great influence in the highest spheres of political power, the senator could help get rid of the extortionists.

Antonym would take Farfarello's advice, and would be told by the politician that he'd only intervene if Hemistich were eliminated—the senator would want to take revenge against he who had blackmailed him. Antonym would hesitate, but Farfarello would convince him it had to be done so they could both be saved, and because of their undertaking. Antonym would then kill Hemistich, after a conversation in which Hemistich would offer himself as a sacrificial lamb. I had a draft of this dialogue, but I lost it. Anyway, after killing Hemistich, Antonym would receive a videotape, delivered to his home. Farfarello had filmed the murder, and would give a copy to the police if Antonym didn't disappear without a trace, leaving the entire business to him, Farfarello.

Disoriented, Antonym would return to the beach, where he'd discovered, or thought he'd discovered, that he was a man of spirit. There, faced with the realisation that he was really no more than a cold-blooded assassin, he'd drown himself.

'Another future dissolved under nature's mantle of silence.' That's the sentence with which I was planning to end the chapter ... What would happen to Farfarello? It would be clear that he had triumphed. Farfarello had masterminded everything: the blackmailing of the senator, Antonym and Hemistich's meeting, Antonym's conversion, the extortionists, the senator's demand that Hemistich be eliminated, Hemistich's murder—and, to an extent, even Antonym's suicide ... No, he wasn't a man of spirit who had chosen the path of Evil. Truth be told, Farfarello was the Devil himself. He had materialised to play with two tiny, pretentious souls—Hemistich's and Antonym's. The name Farfarello, in fact, is a scholarly clue—it is another word for the Devil in early Italian literature.

Go on, ask ... Have I ever believed myself to be a man of spirit, like Antonym? I repeat, I could have chosen to spare my father and myself ... The entirely free will that is an attribute of men of spirit? I know where you're taking this. I'd say I'd be a common criminal if I'd simply killed my father. But my philosophical motives for this act, and for what followed the patricide, belong to the sphere of the extraordinary. I was both the crime and the punishment.

I beg your pardon? No, you're wrong. Someone who kills, then kills himself, is the opposite. The last thing a suicide of this lowly calibre wants is to reap the punishment, do penance for his sin. He's weak. I, on the other hand, am doing penance. I am confronted with my sin every single day.

## 15

I dreamt last night that I was a child and alone at home, feeling sick. I kept on vomiting, and there was no one to help me. Distressing. I did actually find myself in this situation several times, after my mother died. Domestics never lasted more than a year at our place—my father fired them before they got to know us too well. As a result, I was always in the company of strangers who didn't really care whether I was OK or not. They'd do their work, then disappear into the back shed in the afternoons, and they'd only come out to answer the door or fix an afternoon snack ... My routine? I'd go to school in the morning, get home at lunchtime, eat alone, do my homework, watch TV, have afternoon tea alone, go for a swim in the pool, have a shower (I often didn't bother, since no one kept tabs), eat dinner alone, watch more TV, and, when I heard my dad arriving, run to my room to pretend to be asleep. And I would end up falling asleep, obviously.

Whenever I was sick, like in my dream, it was our driver who came to my aid. But he wasn't always at home, since my father used his services a lot. My pre-adolescence was very solitary, as was my adolescence ... Yes, my father took me to doctors about my dizzy spells. They ran a series of tests, which detected nothing. The diagnosis was 'neurovegetative disorder', a name that doctors use when they don't know what the problem is. Since they assured my father that I wasn't going to die from it, he stopped worrying about my crises. I could miss a week of school, and he wouldn't care. He'd go off to work and out on the town, regardless. The only difference on these occasions was that he'd allow his driver to put his other tasks aside and keep me company.

Did I have friends at school? It's not that I didn't, but I was never able to truly be a friend. Every now and then, someone would invite themselves over to my place after school. When this happened, I'd change the subject, or I'd tell them that the pool was being renovated, or that I had a doctor's appointment. Stuff like that. It's hard to explain. I didn't like being alone but, at the same time, I was used to solitude. It seemed to be my natural state … Weekends? Well, when my father was out of town—and he was gone a lot—I'd keep to the same routine as every other day. When he was in town, we'd go to the country club. He'd spend the whole time drinking whisky with his friends, while I'd wander from one group of kids to the next, without settling into any of them.

No, my father had no family. I mean, he did, but he didn't like having contact with them. He came from humble origins, and was irked by the fact that his relatives hadn't broken out of the poverty cycle which had scarred him in his childhood. Actually, when I say relatives, I'm referring to cousins, aunts, and uncles. Both sets of grandparents, on my father and mother's side, died before I was born; and his only brother, who was younger than him, had gone off to Australia without a trace. This uncle once tried to re-establish contact by phone, but my father had chased him off with swear words, according to the driver, who'd witnessed the scene ...

My mother's sister? Well, like I said, she lives abroad. She's lived in several places: New York, Paris, Milan. She went because her husband, an executive with a multinational, was transferred around a lot. After he died, she moved to a small municipality an hour out of Rome, in the mountains — Anticoli Corrado. It's very popular among sculptors and painters. This aunt of mine always had artistic inclinations. She makes etchings; some are interesting. Occasionally, she sends letters — which I don't answer — and tries to get me on the phone, but I don't take her calls. She feels a bit guilty for everything that's happened ... I could talk to her, I know, but the price I've imposed on myself is high. That's the way it has to be.

## 16

When my mother was still alive, I read to acquire enough knowledge to impress her and humiliate my father. When she died, I abandoned my books for a good while. I only went back to them when I was about fourteen. I think I started reading again because it was a more efficient way to pass the time. I read so voraciously that, instead of toys and junk food, I used my hefty allowance to buy books. My father always gave me a lot of money. Not out of generosity, but insouciance. It was a way of saying, *To hell with it. Let him look after himself.* I had to start my collection almost from scratch, since one of the first things my father did when my mother died was donate most of her books to a charity—just as he did her clothes, jewellery, and all her other belongings. Even her photographs ended up with my aunt. I got them back as an adult, and keep them in the cupboard I have here.

I spent my adolescence reading—not least because it irritated my father, who blamed it for the fact that I'd turned into a skinny, pale teenager. At the country club, he couldn't hide his envy of his friends who had strong, suntanned sons who'd already had a string of girlfriends, and who engaged in vile banter. To further set myself apart from them, I opened my mouth only to say that the days of the bourgeoisie were numbered, and that the only thing worse than robbing a bank was founding a bank. Not that I was some snot-nosed wannabe communist. I'd read the *Communist Manifesto*, and other nonsense of that sort, just to have ammunition when I wanted to provoke my father and his rich friends. It was more or less like wearing torn trousers and dirty t-shirts, which I also did.

Concerned that I wasn't like the idiots he considered models of healthy youth, my father decided to, in his words, 'help me become a man'. He started bringing up smutty subjects, and one night dragged me off to a 'special restaurant'—an upmarket brothel. 'Take your pick, and I'll pay,' he said, showing me the girls. To get out of it, I pretended I was dizzy, really dizzy, and that I'd faint if I stayed. My father obviously didn't fall for it. He only agreed to leave because he didn't want to risk becoming a supporting actor in a ridiculous fainting scene. On the way home, he hurled insults at me. He said I was a poof, abnormal, sick, and that he'd never go out in public with me again. Not even to the country club.

To my immense satisfaction, he kept his word. We only went out together again when I started seeing the woman I eventually married ... How old was I when I lost my virginity? It was after my father tried to initiate me—I was about seventeen and a half. I went by myself to a downtown brothel. The whore I chose had a broken arm, and after we had sex, to complete the hour I'd paid for, she started telling me a weird story. She said that where she came from, there were women who gave birth to children who were half human, half animal. She must have been crazy.

Coming back to my reading ... I read so much that it affected my performance at school. I neglected my studies to concentrate on novels, short stories, and plays—some of them impenetrable to a teenager ... Did my books make me happy in any way? On the contrary, they helped me to become even unhappier. But it was a special unhappiness; that of one who believes himself better than others. Turning to books to make oneself feel especially unhappy—there's nothing uncommon about that. I'd even go so far as to say that it makes the most sense. I don't want to dwell much on this, because it's not our topic. I'd just like to say one thing: I think literature confirms human unhappiness for those who are already prone to it. Or, at least, it shows how limited happiness can be. It's possible to compose beautiful symphonies overflowing with the purest joy, and to paint magnificent canvasses in which radiant morning light is the only protagonist. But there is no great book whose main subject is not unhappiness ... Why is that? Because one must be unhappy, in essence, to write a book, and to seek, in the interregnum of writing, some happiness. Clarice Lispector, remember? And me.

The ironic thing is that, because of my devotion to books, I ended up living the illusion that I could be happy full-time. It is an indirect association, but it can be made. They—books—led me to the place where I was to meet my wife ... No, I don't think the expression 'ex-wife' is more appropriate. It's true that we live far apart, but on paper we're still married. From a legal point of view, it was the best way our lawyers could find for me to continue to avail myself of a share of my father's fortune, which is now limited to the payment of my monthly fees here. As I'm sure you know, I lost all right to any direct inheritance when I murdered him.

I can, therefore, call her my wife. And I will do so until the end of my days.

## 17

It was in Paris. I'd finished a degree in philosophy, and bought a place in a Master's program at one of the best universities in France — not only to broaden my horizons, but also to get even further away from my father. He now liked to get his kicks speculating about my future as an unemployed philosopher who was — and this was even funnier, in his opinion — dependent on a capitalist pig who was making fabulous profits in the financial markets. My father was never very original in his jokes, like most capitalist pigs who make fabulous profits in the financial markets. And I, an unemployed philosopher without a future and the son of a capitalist pig, was annoyed by his hackneyed jokes. Anyway, this dependence was easier for me to swallow from a distance of ten thousand kilometres.

Since I was receiving a hefty allowance, I'd rented a flat at a fashionable address on the Left Bank, near the Musée d'Orsay. I attended university in the mornings, and had my afternoons and evenings free. To keep up with the course, all one had to do was read the books on the compulsory reading list, which wasn't too extensive, and that was it. This business of Masters' studies in France is a piece of cake. In my free time, I went to the National Library, where I caught up on French and Russian literature. Their translations of Russian authors are good, except for a few cosmetic interventions to polish up passages that must have been rather dusty.

Once a week, I went out to dinner with my aunt and her husband, who were based in Paris at the time. I'd already been living the good life for about three months when, one winter afternoon, I was approached by the woman who was to become my wife. I was enjoying an essay on Dostoyevsky, when I heard a husky voice — of a promising huskiness — behind me. 'Such concentration!' I turned around, irritated by my fellow-countrywoman's bad manners. But instead of saying something impertinent, I froze.

I don't know if you got to see a picture of my wife in the newspapers during the sensationalist maelstrom that followed my father's death ... No? Well, I'll describe her. It won't be difficult, because she's calendar-girl beautiful. She's tall, with light-brown hair — always cut shoulder-length (I imagine she still wears it like that) — blue-grey eyes, and immaculately white skin. Her body is so perfect that the tiny imperfections a sharp eye may detect here and there only accentuate the harmony of the whole — it is an attribute of beauty to have flaws that, in the context of the whole, only increase the effect of what is beautiful. Her smile, with teeth aligned by orthodontics, is the smile of the middle class, but tempered by a tomboyish air that permeates all of her expressions. Equally delightful is the grace of her movements: the slight sway of her hips as she walks; the gaze that arrives a split-second after she turns to look at someone; and the hands, with long, thin fingers that, when they reach to touch something, move at such a leisurely pace that the world seems to spin more slowly ... Obviously, these last attributes only became evident later. But it was as if I had anticipated all of them the moment that I saw her at the library … Love at first sight? Yes. For lack of a less vulgar definition, that will do.

Since I didn't say a thing, dumbstruck as I was, she started talking to me. She told me that she'd had her eye on me for a week. 'The first time I saw you, you were holding a book by a Brazilian author. That's why I figured that you were …' she explained. She was in the library to research eighteenth-century French cuisine for an essay she had to write for the cooking school she'd been attending for a year. The school was one of the most highly respected in the world, but I guessed that most of the students were rich kids from the Third World who were only there to justify a prolonged stint in Europe. When I put this to her, she protested. She said that when she graduated, she was going to open an ultra-posh restaurant. 'Ultra-posh' isn't in my vocabulary—it's one of my wife's favourite adjectives. Only after telling me all her plans did she ask me what I did. I said I was studying philosophy; but, as I told her about my life, I got the impression she wasn't all that interested. It's curious that, even after our years of life together, this impression hasn't disappeared.

We left the library and headed for a café in Montmartre, where we stayed until the old waiter who was serving us kicked us out. She chattered non-stop; I listened in absolute ecstasy. She told me almost her entire life story. I'd never been out with a woman like this, nor did I understand why a woman like this would be at all interested in me. In the metro, we exchanged phone numbers. We met again, two days later, at a bistro near my flat. She showed up wearing a very expensive fur coat. I was both impressed and ashamed: I still dressed like a sloppy student. During dinner, she made a delicate reference to my apparel. She said that, although I was a philosopher, concerned with ideas and systems, I should pay more attention to my attire. 'Not least because your beautiful watch doesn't go with the clothes you wear.' She was referring to an expensive watch my aunt had given me as a graduation present. Then she suggested we go shopping together the following day. Since this was an opportunity to see her again, I agreed with enthusiasm.

After that, I never stopped buying clothes. Until we left Paris (and we lived there together for four years), we renewed our wardrobes twice a year. We spent a fortune on clothes, on eating out at fashionable restaurants, on furniture, and on indoor decorating. She adored my flat (it really was adorable), but said it needed to be revamped. 'Revamp' is another of her favourite words. Once my flat and I had been revamped, I was introduced to her friends. The group consisted of two Frenchmen, an Italian girl, and an American guy. The first three were also studying cooking. The American was a financier with a large corporation. Since he treated her with more intimacy than was reasonable for friends, she was obliged to confess that they used to be lovers. 'Don't worry, it's completely over,' she assured me.

We started living together four months after we met—not only out of affinity, but also out of necessity. Her expensive habits, the cooking school, and the exorbitant rent she paid for a flat near the Champs-Élysées had consumed much of the inheritance she'd got from her parents, who'd been killed two years earlier in a plane crash. So I invited her to live with me. I was rewarded with one of the most incredible nights of sex in all my life. She was great in bed. She was uninhibited, and liked to be cursed and have her hair pulled. I was no big deal, but she made me feel fantastic ... I beg your pardon? Yes, the idea for the restaurant in *Future* was inspired by my wife's connection with gastronomy. It was she who introduced me to the history of food, and urged me to read a few books on the subject.

Did you know that it was only in the early nineteenth century that books on food lost their pharmaceutical slant and began to concentrate on the palate? The word 'gastronomy', in fact, first appeared in this era. One of the reasons for this is that the sense of taste was highly associated with the sin of gluttony. In other words, it wasn't a topic that authors could explore without guilt. There were even philosophers who considered the sense of taste, like the sense of smell, inferior, given its enormous subjectivity. According to these same thinkers, sight, touch, and hearing were superior, because they allowed one to perceive nature objectively. As you can see, my character Hemistich subverts this philosophical conception by holding taste superior to all the other senses.

At this point, so you don't get the wrong idea, I should make an observation: my wife introduced me to futility, but also to a kind of culture I didn't know. The culture of surface. I'm not talking about polish, or broader general knowledge. The culture of surface ... how can I explain it? The culture of surface is the culture of those who have the intelligence to delve deeper, but are smart enough not to. My wife is well versed in the literary classics, she knows how to tell a good painting from a bad one, she can talk with authority about directors who saw hermeticism as an opportunity to make art out of cinema, but ... But she has never allowed herself to be gripped by intellectual anxiety. It's a voluntary act, hers, not a sign of incapacity. It's not about anti-intellectualism, because she knows how important it is to cultivate the spirit, seeing as she always has. By not allowing herself to be gripped by intellectual anxiety, she filters from philosophy and art that which she considers worth applying to life. That, in my opinion, is called wisdom. A certain kind of wisdom. It was what made her, in my eyes, even more desirable.

She did the same with existential anxieties, per se. Take the death of her parents, for example. She didn't like to remember the accident, and didn't talk about them much. When I tried to talk about her family, she'd sidestep the subject, saying how important it was to forget in order to live. She took this lesson from the best philosophical tradition, incidentally. As for my own family problems, she tried to get me to adopt the same approach: forgetting. Her tactic was to attenuate the dramatic colours with which I painted certain events in my life so they would fade away and eventually disappear. It is true that the facts have proved her wrong in my case. But, even so, she's managed to survive it all well. Very well. Thanks to her approach to life.

Coming back to our story in Paris ... After I met her, my expenses went up so much that it caught my father's attention. He called one morning when I was still in bed with my wife. I started to shake when I heard his voice, as if I'd been caught committing a crime — the crime of being happy. Without asking if I was OK, without any other formality of the sort, he said straight off that I was spending too much. He wanted to know the reason for such a change in my expenditure. Since I was gagging, my wife took the phone. She introduced herself in a very friendly way—'Hi, I'm the spendthrift who's taking you to bankruptcy'—and struck up a conversation in which, as she had done with me at the library, she told him her life story, revealed her plans, and even discussed aspects of her personality. She also described how she looked. I was taken aback by the casual way she was talking to my father. They seemed like old friends. The conversation must have lasted an hour, and ended with laughter. Finally, my father asked to speak to me. 'Very friendly, your wife. She's worth spending money on. I want to meet her. Send me a photo,' he said, and hung up. 'Your father can't be the insensitive monster you've made him out to be,' she said, as she took off her clothes to get into the shower.

I sent my father a photo of my wife. Two weeks later, I received a substantial increase in my allowance. And a message: 'You've finally done something right.'

## 18

I didn't know what to make of this telephonic rapport between my wife and my father. At times I felt peeved that I'd done something which pleased him (being with a woman he judged friendly and beautiful); at others, I thought I should put an end to our battles — and my wife seemed an excellent candidate to foster this family reunion. But, regardless of my feelings, it seemed strange that they should both inhabit the same planet. Although I was dependent on my father, I'd kept him separate from my life in Paris. Allow me to explain: it was as if my existence was a filing cabinet with many drawers. There was the drawer for the 'mother' file, which I wish had been much bigger; another for the 'father' file, which I wish had been smaller; another for the 'philosophy' file; another for the 'literature' file; another for the 'love' file; and so on ... Yes, I'd compartmentalised my life more than was desirable, and for this reason the files hadn't yet come into contact with one another ... OK, you're right, the 'mother' and 'father' files used to be the same ... In a way, the fact that my wife and father got along so well in their first contact showed me that life can't be compartmentalised — it is a futile operation. But it didn't please me in the slightest.

It wasn't long before my father decided to visit us in Paris. My wife insisted that we pick him up from the airport. When I saw him coming from the arrival hall, all of my feelings of inferiority came to the fore. No matter how well dressed I was, I'd never be like my father. As I've already mentioned, he was an attractive man. Taller than me, with an athletic build, tanned (and wearing an overcoat that had been custom-made by a tailor in New York), his mien impressed my wife. When she held out her hand to shake his, she narrowed her eyes slightly, as if making sure he really was made of flesh and blood. We dined with him in one of the most expensive restaurants in town, and I kept noticing tiny alterations in her, including sudden blushes. Her eyes shone, for example, when, after checking the wine list, he made some observations about certain years, winemaking regions, and so on.

My father was really a well of ignorance, but he could be quite deceptive about this by choosing topics that lent him an appearance of refinement, not least because he spoke English and French fluently. I was annoyed, of course, that my wife had been impressed by these things. I tried to bring him down a notch, saying how the nouveau riche in our country liked to pose as wine connoisseurs instead of trying not to be so stupid in more important matters. I have to admit, he handled the provocation well. When the wine was served, he made a toast to tolerance, 'The true sign of intelligence.' My wife laughed, and said that she'd been trying to teach me about wine since we'd met, but I'd refused to learn. 'As if knowing about wine could make his heavy bourgeois conscience any worse,' she said.

Naturally, I had a jealous fit when we were alone again in our flat. I told my wife that if she found him so delightful and refined, she could go and screw my 'old man' (I used this expression, which would normally never come out of my mouth, to bring him down). Since she didn't say anything, I added that we were finished. She let her black silk dress fall to the floor, walked over to me, wrapped her arms around my neck, and whispered that she'd merely found my 'old man' (she knew using the expression would win her points) nice, and that I was only behaving like that because his presence had stirred up my complex. She finished by whispering in my ear, 'The one sleeping with mummy now is you, my love.' We tumbled into bed, kissing passionately. You can imagine how amazing that night was … No, you can't.

My father stayed in Paris for about twenty days. I managed not to be unpleasant the entire time. After all, it was I who was sleeping with mummy now. This expression had a pacifying effect on me—and my wife never tired of using it every night when we got home after dropping my father off at his hotel. Since it also aroused her, it was one of the most ardent periods in our relationship. So much so, that I didn't much mind letting her and father wander the city without my company. My excuse was that he'd come at a time when I—who was always lackadaisical about my studies—had a lot of essays and reports to write. Busy as I was (or wanted to appear to be), I almost always met them at the restaurant where we'd planned to eat. Of course, I felt jealous when I saw that they'd had a perfect day, visiting an exhibition or shopping in Place Vendôme. It was as if my father was taking the opportunity to steal my delightful day-to-day life with her. But I quickly suppressed my jealousy with the thought that the cost–benefit ratio was excellent:

I didn't have to see my father most of the time and, to make up for all the hours she spent with him, my wife exceeded herself in the arts of lovemaking.

At our last dinner, as a way of thanking her for all her attention, my father gave her a diamond ring. 'You make me happy by making my son happy,' he said. Her eyes filled with tears. And, I confess, so did mine.

## 19

My father returned to Paris twice after that. We didn't grow any closer, but a certain cordiality was established, which was my wife's doing. She bent over backwards for him, which included serving as a buffer when I occasionally lashed out, and vice-versa. In exchange, my father gave us more and more money. I even went so far as to think—believe it or not—that this was his way of showing affection. Not that it wasn't, actually ... Would I describe my father as needy? I've never thought about it. As I'm sure I've already mentioned, he was always surrounded by women: all beautiful, all fascinated by his looks, all with an eye on his money. Some were even invited to our house, which must have given them hope that they were on their way to landing a good catch. But, just as he did with our domestics, he'd get rid of his girlfriends as soon as he saw signs that they were getting too close. I don't think my father's longest relationship lasted much more than six months ...

Do I think my father used women? I don't think you gave that question enough thought. What does it mean to use a woman? Generally, when you say so-and-so used a woman, it's to criticise him for not using her for the rest of eternity, or at least for many years. Because this issue of using women is purely an issue of time ... What I mean is that when a woman feels used, it's because, when all's said and done, she doesn't feel she's been used enough. In other words, the phrase doesn't make the slightest sense.

I will try to proceed based on your poorly phrased question. Let's just say that my father liked female company, up to a point. I believe that, during the brief time in which he was with a woman, he loved her. But this love quickly died, not least because of his reluctance to get married again and, consequently, to lose his freedom … The freedom to have other women, you say. Possibly, but I'd like you to try to forget, for a moment, the attitudes that women have established during their long history of resentment towards men. When I said that my father didn't commit to a woman for fear of losing his freedom, I was thinking of something much more banal: the freedom to come and go, without having to answer to anyone. To go to the end of the street, or to Moscow. There is a tendency among women, stronger in some than in others, to control their partners' every move. This makes men's daily lives suffocating. It may even be what makes men become bigger liars, and more deceitful.

Some guys lie not so they can cheat on their wives, but just to get a little fresh air. I read a biological explanation for this several years ago. Women are genetically hard-wired to try to control the men they consider their own. In the past, they did so for fear of losing their reproducers/providers to other women. When a woman was of child-bearing age, or had offspring to feed, such a loss could place her in a situation of social or natural risk. This biological fact, so deeply rooted in modern women, also explains why, as they grow older, they tend to loosen their grip on their partners.

Heading towards infertility, and with no offspring to raise, they no longer need reproducers/providers ...

You weren't familiar with my misogynistic side? Nor was I ... You didn't expect to hear so many clichés issuing from my mouth? My dear, how often are we surprised by what we say, and how often does something that seems intelligent in thought sound frivolous when spoken out loud? But, anyway, you shouldn't underestimate the reach of clichés. The overwhelming majority of people live by them as if they were absolute reality — which, obviously, doesn't make them transcendental truths. Do you know what's just occurred to me? That the clichés in which people imprison themselves are a manifestation of Evil. They ensure that those who become entangled in them do not aspire to elevate their spirit in the slightest; if they did, they might learn, among other things, that Evil itself is part of a higher plan. What I mean is that clichés are among the favourite garments of what we traditionally refer to as the Devil — the fallen angel who wants to be recognised as Evil, but is just a piece of it. I'd like to elaborate on this.

That's an interesting observation of yours: as I tried to work out why my father dumped all his girlfriends, I saw him with loving eyes. Well, that was one of the reasons I killed him. In order to love him.

After almost three years of married life in Paris, I also began to feel asphyxiated by my wife. She was still delightful, but the fact that my day-to-day life was dictated by her pace was no longer such a joy. It was with a certain glee, therefore, that I received the news that she had to spend a month here in Brazil. I was notified of her trip a week before she left, and it took me by surprise. She said she had to resolve some outstanding matters regarding a second inheritance she'd received—this time, from a homosexual uncle who'd died single and left a few assets to his only niece.

On my own, I contacted my aunt, whom I hadn't seen much since I'd met my wife. Their dislike for one another had begun with their first meeting. After that, we still had dinner together—my aunt, her husband, my wife, and I—another two or three times, but this only served to exacerbate their differences. In short, my aunt thought we'd rushed into things. As for my wife, she was smart enough to realise that my aunt had reservations about her.

The fact that my aunt didn't like my wife irked me, but it didn't stop me from thinking highly of her. So much so that I called her a week after my wife had left. We arranged to have dinner together the following night at an elegant bistro. When I arrived at the restaurant, my aunt and her husband were already there. They both looked quite upset—it seemed as if I'd walked in on an argument. The signs were clear: my aunt was shaking, while he was sweating so much that he had to excuse himself to go to the toilet. Before he got up, he looked daggers at her. While he was gone, I took the opportunity to ask what had happened, but all she said was that it was nothing serious; just a little quarrel, like so many others. At first, I believed that that was all it was—a little quarrel—but, because the tension didn't ease up, no matter how I tried to lighten the atmosphere, I started thinking that something more serious had happened.

This impression was confirmed by the odd way she said goodbye to me outside the restaurant. She was making a great effort not to cry, and gave me a more loving hug and kiss than the situation called for. When she hugged me, she whispered in my ear, as if confiding a secret, 'No matter what happens, remember I'll always be there for you.' That was the last time I saw her. Two months later, she and her husband moved to Milan, where he later died.

## 20

I didn't take what my aunt said too seriously. On my way home, I mulled over what had happened at dinner, and I put it all down to a simple emotional crisis. My aunt and her husband were undoubtedly dealing with the anxieties of middle age; even the happiest marriages can go through rough patches during this period. She was probably asking herself if she really wanted to spend the rest of her days with him, I thought, and vice-versa. I could even imagine her dilemma. Her husband had given her a dream life from a material point of view, and still did. He was also fairly intellectually refined, and had always supported her artistic pursuits, bankrolling exhibitions at prestigious galleries, and showing pride in her woodcuts.

Nevertheless, from what I could tell, they didn't enjoy true intimacy, even though they'd been together for many years. It was hard to believe they knew what was going on in each other's heads, given the degree of formality with which they treated one another. I don't know if this was too hasty a conclusion; nor do I know if a man and a woman, regardless of how much they love one another, can be transparent with each other. Perhaps the idea that it's possible is no more than a romantic fantasy. Perhaps I'm too influenced by my own past, in which there was never such transparency—but the fact is that my aunt and her husband always behaved, in my eyes, like two strangers who find themselves having to share a ship's cabin and, though they discover they are similar in many ways, seek to maintain their individual privacy at all costs, hoping for the voyage to end quickly. So much so that they never had kids, even though they both seemed to like children. When I heard that they were moving to Milan, I was sure of one thing: my aunt didn't like the idea of having to leave Paris. The phrase, 'No matter what happens, remember I'll always be there for you' was coming from someone who was about to leave and was not at all happy about it.

Isn't it funny how we can turn logic into a house of cards?

After fifteen days, the solitude was starting to get to me. I didn't yearn for my wife, but I missed her. I'll try to explain the difference. Yearning is fuelled by affection, love, friendship. Missing, on the other hand, is pure and simple, and can be fuelled by feelings that aren't necessarily warm. For example, a torturer can miss inflicting torture, or the opposite: the victim can miss his or her torturer. Not that my wife tortured me; far from it. But I'd grown accustomed to serving her—the voluntary servitude that La Boétie speaks of ... Sorry? I didn't catch that. Could you say it again, please ... Did I, as the tortured one in my relationship with my father, miss my torturer? You've touched on something I've thought about many times, without coming to any conclusion. I gave my father a wide berth, because I couldn't handle being around him, and he did the same with me. But maybe you could say our mutual hatred was so great that

I didn't need to be in his presence to feel tortured, and he didn't need to have me in front of him to torture me.

The money he gave me, for example, was a highly effective instrument of torture, even from ten thousand kilometres away, since I knew that in his mental accounting he considered it a write-off. My father and I only had to know that the other existed in order for our hatred (like everything else that emanated from him) to live on ... You're right, we fed off it ... Go on, ask. I promise I won't be angry ... In my relationship with my father, were our positions ever reversed, and did I ever become the torturer? I've already mentioned that when I was a child I tried to humiliate him in front of my mother, playing the know-it-all—I think that's a form of torture, don't you? ... You want to know if, afterwards, I ever tortured or tried to torture him in any other way? I killed him. Is that enough for you?

I think we'd best end this session.

## 21

I can't get your question out of my head. I knew you were astute, but not that astute. I feel cornered by you—but cornered in a nice way, because I needed this confession. I'm not sure if torture is exactly the right term for what I did to my father in my late teens. Let's just say that I put him through a lot—and took great pleasure in it.

Remember how I told you that my father once took me to an upmarket brothel? Well, worried that I might be homosexual (or, rather, worried about the prospect of having a homosexual son), he decided to take me to see a psychologist. This idiotic suggestion came from his girlfriend at the time, who saw it as a chance to strengthen her ties with him. It didn't work, of course—the girlfriend's attempt to reel him in, I mean. It wasn't long before he gave her the boot. My visits to the psychologist, however, yielded my father a month of desperation.

He announced that he'd made an appointment for me. When I said that I wasn't going, he threatened to cut my allowance. So I went. The psychologist was a young woman of about twenty-five. I could tell she was inexperienced by the hesitant way she asked me questions. In fact, as I found out later, this psychologist had only just graduated and was an old schoolfriend of my father's girlfriend. Not exactly the best resumé. Add to that the fact that I, almost ten years her junior, seemed twenty years older, perhaps because of all my reading and my continuing battle with my father. It was a perfect scenario for revenge. And revenge I got, with the help of a manual by a youth psychologist that my bookseller had recommended.

I followed the script with thespian diligence. In the beginning, I acted withdrawn, like any troubled teenager who finds himself confronted with a psychologist. Then I started alternating between moments of silence and short sentences, in which I sketched out the story of my childhood and my mother's death. Around the fourth week, I started peppering the things I said with crying fits. To be honest, I didn't cry. I buried my face in my hands, and put on a shaky voice. I rubbed my eyes a lot to make them red before looking back at the psychologist. Following what she'd learned at university, she avoided asking why I was crying. This was something she had to unearth on her own, from what was, supposedly, the wreckage of my distant memory—a practice also recommended by the manual that I was following to a T in the chapter that dealt with how some patients cover up their traumas. These manuals really are very useful.

Anyhow, after a month of sessions, the young psychologist was already sufficiently captivated by what appeared to be her first big case. And what a case she had on her hands! In a particularly poignant session, in which I almost wept real tears, I started talking about a monster that used to appear in my room when I was a child, and lie down next to me. And about how, paralysed by fear, I was unable to stop it from touching and biting me. You can see where I was going with this, of course. In the next session, I put the monster to one side, even though she seemed pretty anxious for me to get back to it. Avoiding the core of the trauma, as I learned in the manual, was common among patients — and I was determined to be an exemplary patient. I only mentioned the monster again some four sessions later, throwing in a few sordid details, such as how it used to stroke me and moan in my ear as it did so. It didn't take much — just over two months of therapy — for my psychologist to start to suspect that I'd been sexually abused as a child. And most likely by my father.

I have to say, she was pretty limited ... No, she didn't reveal her conclusions to me. The person who did reveal them was my own father, which for me only enhanced the flavour of my revenge. It played out like this: first, she invited him down for a private interview. She started the conversation by asking him if I'd had a vivid imagination as a child. My father, of course, didn't know what to say. Then she asked if another man had lived with us when I was young: an uncle, or an employee perhaps. My father said 'no', and that after my mother's death he'd hired a driver, but only recently had he come to live in a shed behind our house. She also asked him about his feelings towards me — if, at any time, for example, he'd wished that I hadn't been born, or things like that. My father must have really got his tongue in a twist at this point. Finally, the psychologist told him that she'd need to have him back for another interview. When he asked her why, all she said was that she couldn't explain anything at that moment.

The second time he went back, he found himself meeting

the psychologist's supervisor, whom I'd met two weeks earlier in a particularly difficult session. She was a woman of about sixty, with a respectable, intimidating air about her. She played the devil's advocate, questioning everything I said; but, by this time, I was so into my 'abused child' role that my performance would have convinced all the members of the Vienna Psychoanalytic Society in Freud's day. It was in the interview with her, which lasted nearly two hours, that my father was informed that there were strong signs I'd been molested by him as a child. This explained my withdrawn, unaffectionate behaviour towards him — though the lack of affection appeared to be reciprocal, as my psychologist and her supervisor had gathered from the things he'd said about me. And this, they'd concluded, could be considered further proof that something very serious had fractured our relationship.

My father tried to argue that it was all rubbish, and that if he was guilty of something like that he'd never have sent me for psychological counselling, which he'd done precisely because he suspected I was having problems with my sexual orientation. They were both unyielding in their conviction. His argument might have worked a month earlier — but by this stage they'd picked up too many signs of something very strange having happened between my father and me. Do you know how the supervisor answered my father? 'The fact that you took the initiative in seeking psychological counselling for your son is indeed strange. But, just as the reasons that lead a criminal to return to the scene of a crime are apparently fathomless, the motives that led you to bring your boy to my colleague's practice are only inexplicable on the surface. I am referring to your subconscious, sir.'

When he told me, at the top of his lungs, what had happened at the psychologist's practice, I had to make a great effort not to laugh. Not least because his girlfriend, who was watching the scene, had such an expression of shock on her face. The specialist in psychological torture had got a taste of his own medicine. I'd suffered because of the story that I was adopted; now it was his turn to feel desperate. I'd show him who the weak one was … What was my response? That I'd told the psychologists about my childhood feelings and fears, and that it wasn't my fault if his girlfriend's friend had made that assumption. I shot the girlfriend a look of contempt. 'The funniest bit is that you sent me to see a psychologist because you thought I was a poof. And now you're the poof—a poof who used to fuck his own son,' I said, unable to suppress a mocking smile. When he heard that, he flew at me. I leapt back, while his girlfriend tried to hold him off. 'Don't—you're only going to make things worse,' she kept saying. I managed to escape to my room, and locked myself in, cackling with laughter. I was avenged.

How did it all end? Weeks after this scene, my father's girlfriend showed up at our place, alone, and asked if she could talk to me in my room. She said that since I kept remembering vile details about the monster who used to appear in my room to fondle me, her psychologist friend and the supervisor were thinking about contacting a family court judge, because the case was beyond their jurisdiction. She explained that a court order would probably be issued to strip my father of custody of me. Additionally, criminal charges would certainly be brought against him, and he might even go to jail. 'You're going to destroy your father. So think hard about what you're doing. If it helps, he doesn't know I'm here, nor did he ask me to talk to you. This was on my own initiative,' she said.

My father's girlfriend was a brunette of about twenty-four, give or take a few years, and very attractive. I'd already masturbated a couple of times thinking about her—especially her breasts, with her nipples always sticking out because she never wore a bra. When I saw her there in my room, begging me to save my father's hide, I couldn't resist the temptation to give my revenge a grand finale. I said I'd tell the psychologists that the story about the monster wasn't true if she agreed to have sex with me. I expected her to act as if I'd offended her honour, but she surprised me. She locked the door and took off her blouse, jeans, and high-heeled sandals. Wearing just her knickers, she lay down on the bed. 'Come,' she said. So I went.

The poof, the freak, the sicko, after sullying his dad's reputation, had lost his virginity with his dad's girlfriend. Sweet revenge, you must agree ... No, he never knew what happened with his girlfriend. He died thinking that I'd told the psychologists it wasn't true, to ease my conscience. At least, that's what I think.

Sometimes, I think he did send his girlfriend to talk to me, and that he did know she'd had sex with me. Maybe if I hadn't proposed it, she would have done so herself, as part of a plot hatched by my father. What makes me think that? She didn't seem surprised by my gall, and shortly after I denied everything to the psychologists, saying it had all been a joke, she showed up in a flash car that my father had given her.

But my father wasn't the sort to give his girlfriends expensive presents. What do you think? You don't think anything, I know. I forgot—you can only have opinions when they're of direct interest to you … The crazy whore to whom I was supposed to have lost my virginity? She was real, but she was actually my second.

## 22

Sorry? You're going to terminate our sessions if I don't admit ...
Fine, I admit it: everything I said in the last session was made
up. I didn't go to a psychologist, much less accuse my father of
molesting me. Nor did I have sex with any girlfriend of his.
What made you think I was lying? You're right: such defiance
wasn't in keeping with the weakness I always demonstrated in
my relationship with my father, especially after my mother's
death ... Go on ... If I had confronted him as a teenager, even
if contumeliously, our story—my father's and mine—most
probably wouldn't have taken the fatal turn it did. Right ...

I'm sorry, I only wanted ... Truth be told, even though
the things I told you didn't take place objectively, they did
subjectively. My father only said that he was going to take
me to see a psychologist, but he soon abandoned the idea. To
do it would have shown some kind of concern for me. But,
after he considered taking me for psychological counselling,
I imagined avenging myself in the way I told you ... The
girlfriend? You want to know about the girlfriend? ... Yes,
she existed. I wanted her, like I wanted several of my father's
girlfriends. They were beautiful young women, provocative
in the way they dressed and undressed. We had a swimming
pool, as I mentioned before, and they were always parading
through the back yard in bikinis.

This brunette, in particular, drove me crazy. From time to time, she'd ask me to rub sunscreen on her back ... I'd do it, then run to my room, trying to hide my erection, which continued even after I'd masturbated. When my father dumped her, I thought about going to her, to declare how I felt about her. I fantasised about consoling her in my arms, while I kissed her neck, her mouth, her breasts ... You know, one of the things I remember about my adolescence was hovering outside my father's bedroom door when he was in there with a girlfriend, trying to hear some kind of sound that would indicate they were having sex. A moan, a whisper, a muffled cry—anything. But I never heard a thing, I think, although sometimes my memory suggests I did ...

Go ahead and ask ... What's the first image that comes to mind when I think about my father having sex with a girlfriend? A scene of sodomy, perhaps ... Of a man with an enormous phallus tearing a woman who dared to offer herself to him ... That's the kind of thing you wanted to hear, right? I know your lot. But enough. I'm not interested in interpretations. Indulge in them far away from me, and without my collaboration. What purpose do they serve, for God's sake? Above all, I agreed to tell my story in order to organise it in my own mind, full stop. You're no more than a supporting actor here; do you understand? So don't try to become a protagonist with your interpretations.

Would you like me to go on? Fine. But let's stick to the story, because we're close to the denouement.

My wife returned to Paris after a month's absence. Our reunion was marked by a certain coldness. Not that there wasn't hugging and kissing, but it was as if we were performing a ritual required by a hypothetical protocol. While we were still at the airport, she justified her delay, saying that, because of the extra time she'd had, she'd managed to clear up all outstanding matters with the lawyers handling her uncle's inheritance and, as a result, a considerable amount of money was already in her bank account. During the week that followed, we gradually got back into our Parisian routine. The joy the city had once inspired in us, however, was no longer there. Everything had lost its magic. My wife had already graduated from her cooking course, and I was about to finish my Master's, without a distinction. After it was completed, we travelled in Europe a little, wandered through a few South-East Asian countries in search of some exoticism, and returned to Paris. We spent another year in this limbo, putting off a decision that we knew had already been made: to come back to Brazil.

Why did we come back? It's hard to say. I think that when we have no reason to stay away, we're obliged to content ourselves with the reasonlessness of staying close to our roots. This is, in my opinion, an impulse common to everyone who has gone through the experience of an inexplicable return. I'm speaking for myself, not my wife. But you know what? Maybe she was also seeking a higher reason for this return to our homeland, above and beyond the other reason that made her push a lot for us to come back. I'll get to that later.

The fact is, we came back. We spent the first few months in a rented flat while we renovated and decorated the house that my father had given us as a present, in a neighbourhood near his. My wife, as was to be expected, took great care with every detail, with the help of an architect/interior decorator who pocketed a fortune in commissions from the purchase of materials, furniture, and accessories. The result, of course, was very good. It combined the right proportions of personal touch and design.

When the house was ready, I was surprised by a request from my wife: she wanted us to make our marriage legal. There was, in this, a yearning for social recognition, a need to use the front door in the world of the rich and powerful that was my family's habitat—I mean, my father's. My wife was fascinated by my father's network of friends and contacts. I was dragged off to parties and dinners every night, and was always impressed by her self-assuredness on these occasions. It's true that my wife had never been shy, but her behaviour was a source of constant astonishment to me.

I did and I didn't like it. I'll try to explain: I liked it, because having a wife like mine could be considered irrefutable evidence that I wasn't the weirdo my father made me out to be. If I'd managed to seduce her, it was because I was an interesting man. But, at the same time, I didn't like it, because exposing myself like this might reveal that, contrary to what seducing such a woman indicated, I really wasn't such an interesting man, and maybe was even a weirdo.

Our wedding was a grand occasion, with about one thousand guests, a sumptuous dinner, and photographs in the social columns. My father felt it was incumbent on him to spend an incredible sum on this demonstration of power and prestige. My wife looked stunning in her bridal gown. When she walked into the church, to be given away by my father, who was especially handsome that night, a murmur of admiration ran through the audience. Even I was impressed … How did I feel about the wedding? Anaesthetised. I took part in it all, as if none of it had anything to do with me. It's not that I didn't love my wife; but, at that moment, I was hollow, with nothing inside me. I didn't have good or bad feelings, an intellectual repertoire, nothing. I moved like a robot, responding to outside stimuli with the minimum expenditure of energy — not least because I had none.

This sensation continued through our honeymoon, although I did my best to pretend to be happy. We went to a paradisiacal island, and I spent hours staring at the sea. The sea from which I'd been saved by my father, and in which I now imagined I was dissolving. It wasn't a death wish, because even wishes require some kind of desire. I just thought about being taken away by the water, like a defenceless child. Defenceless — and motherless. I'd never thought so much about my mother as on my honeymoon. I'd never missed my mother as much as I did on my honeymoon. It is curious that, right when a man is most required to prove his manhood, I had become so childlike. I cried in secret, and these tears were so much bitterer because it was more and more difficult to remember the contours of her face, the timbre of her voice.

My wife was too caught up in herself to worry about me. She wasn't even bothered by the fact that we didn't have sex on the occasion specifically made for it. To be honest, I think she felt relieved, since our sex life was no longer (or perhaps never had been) a big deal for her. It may sound paradoxical, but our honeymoon was the moment in which our emotional separation became explicit. We began, there, a marriage of convenience — much more for her than for me.

## –23–

We spent another four years trying to forget we'd taken vows to be together. It was all very schizophrenic: my wife circulated in high society, growing bubblier and bubblier, while I taught night school to a sorry bunch who slept during my classes, tired from the shitty day they'd had. At least I had a good excuse not to go with her to all the dinners and social gatherings she attended. What most irritated me about them was having to spend time in the company of the same idiots whom my father thought had displayed model behaviour back when I was a teenager. They hadn't deviated in the slightest from the road to total stupidity. The only difference was that now they smoked cigars, slopped gel into their hair, and slept with more expensive whores, while their equally futile wives turned a blind eye.

I still didn't have any friends (and, by this stage, never would). As is usually the case with teachers, I could have established friendlier ties with my students. I tried, but they were as devoid of inner life as the wealthy folks with whom my wife loved to rub shoulders. It's amazing how wealth and poverty, by different routes, can have the same effect of emptying people. The only human being in whose company I derived any pleasure was my father's driver—the one who'd helped me, and kept me company so often when I was a child.

He was different from most poor people, which was why I liked him so much. He wasn't complacent, nor did he complain about his lot in life. By that, I don't mean that he was a conformist. He was a realist. He knew how to assess situations in order to make the most of them, or to bow out when necessary. As well, he had no patience for the other employees' moaning and groaning. Whenever he heard someone complaining about being broke, he always made a point of asking them, 'OK, but what have you done to try to earn more money?' I think he would have made a steely executive if he'd had the chance. I once asked him why he hadn't finished his studies. His answer was surprising: 'The cost-benefit ratio is no good. To cover the expenses of night school and a second-rate university, I'd have to work for at least eight years in a job that paid six times what I earn now. But even after completing night school and getting a second-rate university degree, I'd never get a job like that.' It was incredible that a man of the people could be sharp enough not to be sucked in by the nonsensical notion that one had to study to move up in life in a country such as ours. I admired his approach to life, and benefited from it. When I was a child and had my dizzy spells, the driver was always there to try and make me see things as they really were, without the fog of despair ... No, he wouldn't have made a good analyst. You lot usually only make the fog thicker.

My father liked him a lot—not least because he could leave me in his hands on a day-to-day basis. He liked him so much that he invited him and his wife to come and live with us. She took on the role of head housekeeper and, in this position, managed to put a stop to the high turnover of domestics. She taught them to be a reliable, cooperative and, above all, silent team. To paraphrase a butler from the movies, they learned to live as if they didn't exist. I didn't really hit it off with our driver's wife—I sensed in her, from the first instant, a resentment towards the wealthy. At any rate, it was a dislike that had no great bearing on my life, since both she and I avoided saying anything more than was strictly necessary to one another. When she needed to communicate with me, to pass on a message, or something of the sort, she preferred to write notes. I think she was proud of her flowing handwriting and good grammar. Unlike her husband, she'd managed to finish high school. She came from a family of Italian immigrants who'd settled in the countryside—small-time shop owners who'd lost the little they'd managed to make when the economy took a downward turn. In love with her husband, and with no hope of finding a decent job, she'd agreed to run away with him to the big city. It's what I'd call a classically banal story.

Our driver was also valuable to my father because he helped rid him of personal annoyances—things that had nothing to do with me. He was discreet, and never disclosed details about the special services, so to speak, that he carried out for my father. However, from the little I was told, I deduced what they were. For example, my father had him take large sums of money to crooks who specialised in offshore accounts. Another situation in which he was useful was when it became necessary to dissuade a woman from calling my father after he'd dumped her.

You might think it odd that I appreciate a person who was willing to perform such services. But you must remember that we had already formed a bond long before I found out what his other duties were — the sentences of moral judgements tend to be much lighter when preceded by emotional ties. Generally speaking, this is an error we like to make, as if it confirms our humanity. I'd even go so far as to say that emotional ties formed *a posteriori* also serve to dilute negative opinions. You, for example, may no longer judge me as severely as you would have before you met me … We don't have an emotional tie? I'm inclined to think you're mistaken.

Now, where was I? Ah, yes, my marital problems. My wife didn't notice I was unhappy, and I didn't know how to tell her how unhappy I was. It was with some surprise, therefore, that she received the news that I'd decided to start analysis. That night, we had a frank discussion. I told her I couldn't stomach the parties and dinners with those unbearable people, I loathed my job, and I hoped that analysis would help me find a way out of the condition of *artiste manqué*. Yes, because I needed to create something. Maybe write a book. I had some interesting ideas, but didn't feel stimulated enough to organise them — although I'd already tried to do it once, back in Paris, without her knowledge.

She listened to everything in silence. When I finished, she was pensive for a few seconds, then she locked herself in the bathroom. She came out with her face puffy from crying. She gave me a hug, apologised for not paying me enough attention, and said she'd support me in every decision I made. She promised to slow the pace of her social life so she could spend more time with me, and said she'd find herself something useful to do. She asked what I thought about her setting up a catering service, where she could put her Parisian culinary qualifications to good use. I said I didn't have enough money, and would have to ask my father for help once again. Unless, of course, she used the money she'd inherited from her uncle. I noticed that she squirmed a little at the mention of the money. 'I think I'll be able to find an investment partner among those unbearable people you so abhor,' she said. We then gave ourselves over to desperate, sad sex.

## 24

I went to analysis prepared to talk openly about myself, as I do with you. But the conversation took on a less polished, more brutal quality. And, perhaps for this reason, it was insincere. You could call it a paradoxical form of resistance — psychological resistance in this case, of course. My love for my mother, my sadness over her death, my hatred of my father and my awful relationship with him, the difficulties of my marriage, my lack of friends — I dumped all this information on my analyst almost pornographically, as a man dumps his load on his lover's face. She, in turn, was unable to hide her glee at having such a neurotic patient. I was an exemplary case, and learned to behave as such. I was the supreme Narcissus, allowing myself to be autopsied with the instruments of psychoanalysis, but only to a point.

It's not surprising that she became furious with me. She'd hoped for a glorious ending, but I gave her a tragic one. The idiot even talked about my case to the press ... I can't say, however, that it wasn't good for me in some respects — analysis, I mean. Although propelled by narcissism, I started writing *Future* and, with this, began to glimpse the possibility of a literary career. My marriage also seemed to be getting back on track. My wife still went to parties and dinners, but not as often. Her efforts were now focused on opening her catering service. She hadn't found an investment partner, and so was considering using the money from her inheritance. I didn't like this idea—even though I was the one who'd suggested it—but didn't raise any objection. I'd never kept tabs on my wife's finances, nor did I know exactly how much her uncle had left her. I was only worried that she might lose everything on an unsuccessful initiative.

This impasse lasted around two months, until she decided to use the money she'd been left. She was having a meeting in our study with a financial consultant, when I took a peek at the numbers they'd written on a piece of paper. I was surprised. The amount to be spent was much, much more than I'd imagined. 'Where are you going to get that kind of money?' I asked. 'From my inheritance,' she answered. I was even more perplexed, because the amount written there was at least double what she'd once said she'd got from her uncle. I manifested my surprise, and she said I was a philosopher out of touch with reality. 'Do you think I just left the money sitting in the bank? I made excellent financial investments, thanks to my esteemed consultant here. Isn't that right?' she said, turning to the short, bald man beside her, who I wouldn't have known from a bar of soap. Busy with his calculator, he just mumbled, 'Yes.'

On my way to night school, I put it out of my mind. I only had room in my head for Antonym, Hemistich, and Farfarello. The characters in my book had led me to contemplate the abyss of Evil, blinding me to the fact that it, Evil, was taking a form that was to far exceed literature and philosophy. What can I say? My wife was right: I really was a philosopher out of touch with reality. And this was a tremendous philosophical error.

## 25

It was a Saturday afternoon. I was alone at home, writing my book, when the parlourmaid knocked at the study door to announce that my father's driver wanted to talk to me. 'Put the call through,' I said. 'He's in the kitchen, sir,' she replied. The driver wasn't in the habit of showing up out of the blue, so I assumed that something serious had happened. I was right: he had decided to inform me that he and his wife had been fired by my father. 'Your father has accused us of stealing twenty-five thousand American dollars from his safe,' he said, without the slightest emotion.

I was dumbstruck. They were entirely trustworthy. How could he possibly …? 'Your father said he won't go to the police but, on the other hand, he won't give us a penny of severance pay. I'm here to ask for your help. My wife and I need some money for a hotel while we find a place to rent,' he continued, unfazed. His steel was truly impressive. No whining, no tears.

I told him I was very sorry, and that I thought my father had made a huge mistake in accusing him. He didn't say a word to defend himself. At this moment, the driver was a monument to dignity. The only thing I could do was fill his pockets with money, so that's what I did. As well as giving him the American dollars I kept at home — about five thousand—I gave him everything in my wallet, in Brazilian currency. Still not content, I wrote him a cheque for a decent sum, equivalent to about ten months of his and his wife's combined wages.

When he shook my hand to take his leave, I noticed that there were tears in his eyes. For him, this was equivalent to the wailing of a professional mourner. 'Thank you, son. Take care,' he said. Those were the words of a father—the father I'd never had. After he left, I managed to finish the chapter I was writing. The last chapter of *Future*.

I was upset, so I called my father to ask him to explain himself. 'They robbed me; I fired them,' was all he said. I hurled a string of expletives at him. 'And you're just an idiot,' he said, before hanging up on me. When my wife got home, I told her what had happened. All she said was that it wasn't our problem, and that she and I had other things to worry about.

And indeed we did: in less than a week, I received the news that I was going to be a father. We hadn't planned anything, so my wife's nervousness when she told me that she was pregnant seemed quite natural. I didn't know she'd already had a lab test to confirm the result of a home pregnancy test—also done without my knowledge. She cried a lot, saying that it wasn't the right time for us to have a kid; she'd slipped up, and I shouldn't have to pay for her mistake.

Knowing we were having a child really shook me up. I paced the garden, holding the test results, thinking about the irony of becoming a father without ever having stopped becoming a son. What I mean is that I depended on my father more than I should have and, to quote my analyst, I still hadn't managed to grieve for my mother—this had become evident on my honeymoon. Actually, according to her, my hatred for my father would only ease off after I'd managed to grieve ... Let's not, please, go into the merit of these interpretations. The fact is that, at this instant, they made enough sense for me to accept the idea of having a child. This child could mark my entry into the adult world.

I made an extra appointment with my analyst for the next day. She agreed that, with the right psychological counselling, having a child would be very positive for me, but she warned me that it would be a mistake to hold it responsible for whatever came to pass in my life. I left her practice feeling readier than ever for parenting. Before heading home, I stopped at a jeweller's and bought a beautiful diamond necklace for my wife. It was to be her first present as a mother.

When I arrived, I found her sitting on the armchair in our room with the lights out. I switched on a lamp but, before I could speak, she said she'd thought a lot during the night and had come to the conclusion that she should get an abortion. In her opinion, a child would only bring unnecessary problems into our marriage. And she enumerated the ones we already had: we still hadn't fully settled into a stable routine; she was about to open a business that would take up a lot of her time in the beginning; and I had no idea when I was going to finish my book.

My reaction to these rational arguments was to appeal to her emotional side. I said that no one in the history of humanity had ever felt, or would feel, ready to have a child, and that that was what made life so much more fascinating. I also said that a child would be, for me, a reason to push on in the 'desert that had to be cultivated in reverse', to quote João Cabral de Melo Neto. I'd always wanted to adapt the poet's line to a concrete situation, and now the opportunity had presented itself. Then I gave my wife her present, crowning the scene with a line that I'm ashamed to repeat: 'For the most beautiful mother in the world.' When she saw the necklace glittering in the lamplight, she smiled through her tears. She hugged me, saying she'd never disappoint me again.

## 26

My story is drawing to an end and, much as I would like to go on, there isn't much more to say. It's a shame. Spending time with you has done me good ... You've already said that you'll come back whenever you can, I know. But I don't think it's very likely. Do you know how that makes me feel? Like a guide at a nature reserve in Africa. Years ago, I saw a story in a TV documentary that struck a particularly deep chord in me; I can see it has taken on a greater-than-normal importance in my memory. A guide is introduced to a tourist he's going to take on a safari. He shows him the wildlife all around them; the intensive contact makes them grow close; and, at the end, when it's time to say goodbye, the tourist tells the guide that one day they'll meet up again in that very place. The guide, who lives alone, knows from past experience that this won't happen — they all say the same thing. Not that it's a lie, because, at the time, the tourist really does believe he'll come back to the reserve. But the minute that the tourist returns to civilisation, the guide becomes nothing more than a travel memory. I think this story made a mark on me because it reproduces, in the arena of personal relationships, the myth of Sisyphus. The guide is Sisyphus; his stone, the friendships that never come to fruition.

I didn't have time to tell my father face-to-face that I was going to have a child. He'd left the country the day after he fired the driver and housekeeper, and the news of my wife's pregnancy only caught up with him in New York, by phone. It was my wife who rang him. 'I'm calling to tell you I'm pregnant,' she said, and she went completely quiet as she listened to what he said. Then she said, 'Thank you', and passed me the phone. 'You don't deserve a grandson, but that's life—it rewards those who don't deserve it,' I said. My provocation got no response. 'Congratulations,' he answered. And hung up. My wife, who was generally a peacemaker, didn't say a thing about my unpleasant behaviour. She changed her clothes, and went out. 'I need to get some air,' she said.

When I'd farewelled my friend the driver, I'd told him to contact me if he ever needed anything. But I hadn't expected him to do so quite so soon. Later that same afternoon, I received a note, written in his wife's flowing hand and signed by him. 'I need to talk to you. It's urgent. I am staying at a hotel in the centre of town. Below is the address. Please come today.' At first, I thought he wanted more money. But, after giving it a little thought, I came to the conclusion that it didn't make any sense for him to ask me to come to his hotel to ask me for money. I was intrigued, and decided that I would go after dinner.

My wife and I had what was to be our last supper. We were monosyllabic. She didn't speculate as to why the driver had sent the note, and I didn't dwell on it either. After dinner, she went to bed. I even thought about putting off going to the hotel; but, since I had nothing better to do, I went to meet the driver.

One would have assumed that his hotel was modest, bordering on sordid. But it wasn't. It was a four-star hotel, with a lobby flash enough to make me think that the driver and his wife were frittering away their money. I announced my arrival, and was told to wait a little while before going up. I waited thirty minutes, in which time every bit of the class prejudice I'd tried my whole life to stifle flowered in me. Angry, I thought how absurd it was for underlings like themselves to subject me to a humiliating wait, and in the setting of a dodgy little downtown hotel to boot (my anger had already made me notice fluff balls on the lobby carpet, as well as dirty ashtrays and peeling furniture). To show that I'd taken offence, I could have left but, truth be told, I was too curious to find out why the driver needed to talk to me so urgently.

I was finally given permission to go up. It was the driver's wife who opened the door. We greeted one another coldly before she invited me to take a seat. I glanced around the room. My father's former housekeeper was still a stickler for order: there wasn't a wrinkle on the bedspread, their suitcases were closed and stowed out of the way in a corner, and the glasses on the table were washed and standing bottom-up, even though there were two empty soft-drink cans in the rubbish. The driver was in the bathroom for a few minutes before he finally emerged with a startled expression, and sweating a lot. 'It's hot in here, isn't it? I'm going to turn up the air-conditioning,' he said, holding out a limp hand in a way that wasn't natural for him.

Sitting in front of me, with his wife standing beside him, he was still sweating profusely, even with the thermostat set to the minimum temperature. 'Are you feeling unwell?' I asked. 'No, he's afraid,' answered his wife. Then the driver started to cry. You can imagine how awkward I felt. It was the first time I'd ever seen him lose his cool. I told them I didn't understand a thing, and asked them to hurry up and tell me what was going on, so I could see if there was something I could do to help. 'Your father ... He wants us dead,' mumbled the driver.

I hated my father's guts, and knew he was capable of doing the most miserly and dishonest things, but this was too much. I raised my voice to say that a man like my father wouldn't put his social standing in jeopardy to kill some former employees, or to have them killed. Especially because, given the circumstances of their dismissal, if he were to perpetrate a crime like that, all the evidence would point to him. It would be stupid, I concluded, and my father was anything but stupid.

I'd barely finished speaking, when the driver's wife let out a hysterical cackle. 'You rich folks think you're better than us, don't you? So much so that you're prepared to question something we actually heard and witnessed,' she said. Irritated by her insolence, I told her that I thought it very odd they hadn't gone to the police to file a complaint against my father. 'The police work for the rich, not the poor,' she retorted. I said that maybe they hadn't gone down to the police station for a much more concrete reason—the twenty-five thousand dollars stolen from my father. She went bright red and didn't answer, then turned to her husband and shouted that he should just go ahead and tell me everything.

Part of what you're going to hear now isn't in my criminal trial records. I wanted to spare the survivors.

When he heard his wife's order, the driver, who no longer bore any resemblance to the steely, dignified man I had learned to admire, got up, came over to me and, with his face almost touching mine, said, 'Your father and your wife ...'

He didn't finish the sentence, nor did he need to. My head started to spin, like when I was a child. I asked to lie down on the bed, and there I stayed for I don't know how long. I have to say, I didn't feel at all angry—just disappointed. And, curiously, I was more disappointed with my father than my wife. Which meant I must still have had some kind of positive expectation of him, in spite of our history.

When I felt a bit better, I asked the driver's wife to leave the room so I could talk to her husband in private. Then he told me everything he knew.

Their affair had started back in Europe. He was the reason she'd returned to Brazil for a month, leaving me on my own in France. The driver had been assigned to her for her entire stay, taking her shopping and to meet my father. She'd stayed at a hotel, where my father had spent all of his nights. After we returned to Brazil, they continued seeing one another, but with less frequency. The day before our wedding, she'd spent the whole afternoon with him in a motel room. They'd been more distant for a time, but had taken up again about two months ago.

At this point, my heart froze: this meant my wife might be pregnant to my father, and not to me.

My dizziness got worse again, and the whole room spun. I was in a pitiful state but, even so, I managed to keep listening to the driver's story. He told me that, at first, he'd been amazed that my father hadn't tried to hide something so immoral from him. But his wife had a good explanation for this. 'For the rich, we poor folks aren't people. We don't hear anything, see anything, notice anything. We're just beasts of burden,' she'd said.

It was impossible to disagree, seeing that history was replete with powerful individuals who'd got into serious trouble for having underestimated their subordinates. I asked, then, why my father wanted them dead. It all began, the driver said, when his wife decided to blackmail my father. They wanted to move back to her hometown in the country and open a cake shop, but hadn't managed to save up enough money to buy a house there. Having their own business was their dream. After many arguments, she'd convinced him to put the screws on my father by threatening to tell me he was having an affair with my wife. Blackmailed, my father remained impassive. He just went to the safe, took out twenty-five thousand dollars, and handed the money to the driver. 'Now, get lost and never show your face around here again,' he said. The sight of so many dollars, however, had whetted his wife's greed as well as his own. They imagined that, since I hated my father, I'd easily be led to believe he'd been unfair—and so wouldn't hesitate to give them money.

Everything had gone according to plan ... except for one detail. They'd already moved into the hotel when they received a phone call. On the other end of the line, an acquaintance warned them that my father, furious at having been blackmailed, had hired a hit man to kill them. This acquaintance was well connected in the underworld, and had decided to warn them because he was also a bit hard up, et cetera. If there was something in it for him, he added, he could find a way to make sure that the service wasn't carried out. It soon became apparent that this scoundrel was in cahoots with the hit man, whom he probably managed. When asked, in a second call, how much this protection would cost, the guy said my father had offered five thousand dollars, plus the twenty-five thousand in the possession of his former employees. 'But if you pay us twenty-five thousand dollars, you're in the clear,' said the acquaintance, letting out a little chuckle. The crooks' rationale was based on a simple premise: it was better to get less not to kill than to get just a little bit more to kill. The couple had no choice but to pay up—which is what they did.

Since they had nothing else to lose, the driver went on, his wife had said I should be informed of my father's affair with my wife. It was both revenge and a guarantee: my father wouldn't dare hire another assassin after the family scandal blew up. It would be too obvious. The driver had been convinced by his wife's arguments, and there he was, telling me everything. 'We're leaving town tomorrow, and are never coming back. I'm so sorry to let you down, but I had no choice,' he concluded, in tears.

When I left the hotel, it was already well after midnight. I had the phone number of the guy who managed the hit man in my pocket.

My dizziness was gone.

## 27

It was all too vulgar—the fact that my father was having an affair with my wife and, blackmailed by his employees, had hired a hit man to take them out. My own fiction was much better than this slapstick reality. This was the only thing of which I was certain.

I didn't want to head home, because I didn't have the stomach to face my wife. But going to a hotel would be worse. So I decided to lock myself in the study, where there was a sofa bed. I didn't get a wink of sleep, of course. I was disoriented. I needed someone to talk to, but I had no friends. There was just my aunt, who lived in Milan. I called her. I woke her up and, without any preamble, relayed what had happened. There was a long silence on the other end of the line, then she said in a teary voice that she already knew everything. She would have told me at our last dinner in Paris if her husband hadn't stopped her. This was the reason for the argument in the restaurant that had contaminated our evening. I asked her how she'd found out. She said that she'd seen them kissing on a street corner in the Marais district, late one afternoon. They hadn't seen her. Her shock, of course, had been great, and she'd ended up at the doctor's with a bout of hypertension. She repeated that she would have told me, but her husband hadn't let her, for fear that I might do something silly. He'd even threatened to leave her. 'Forgive me, son. Perhaps it would have been better for you to hear it from me,' she said, now bawling. I hung up.

I came out of the study late in the morning. My wife was at the breakfast table. Without responding to her 'good morning', I told her that I knew about everything. 'About what?' she asked. 'That you and my father are having an affair,' I said, helping myself to some coffee, as if it was all very natural. I continued with my breakfast while, on her knees, she cried, begging for forgiveness. I could retell the scene in dramatic colours, but it was just pathetic.

After she stopped crying, I ordered—yes, ordered—her to give me the details. She said that she'd succumbed to my father's charms back in Paris, and that her trip back to Brazil had been to see him. 'There was no inheritance?' I asked. 'No,' she answered. I asked how she'd got the money to open her catering service, even though I already knew the answer. She confirmed that my father had given it to her, and told me the rest of the story. She said that he'd put pressure on her to return to Brazil, threatening to cut the money he sent us. She'd tried everything possible to end the affair, and the idea of us getting legally married had been an attempt to create an obstacle to his advances.

However, she went on, when he heard we were getting married, he started acting sadistically. He demanded that she spend the afternoon at a motel with him on the day before. 'If you don't, I'll tell my son everything,' he threatened. After the wedding, my father had made several other attempts to rekindle things, but their encounters had been rare, until they'd stopped completely. 'But you started seeing him again two months ago,' I said, when I realised that her long silence was a full stop. She rubbed her eyes, took a deep breath, and said that she'd made this mistake because she needed the money. She really did want to open a catering service, and didn't have any other way to raise the capital, except by placing herself at my father's mercy. 'Even if you'd asked him for the money, he would have come to me for reimbursement in the form of sex. So I thought it was better to ask him myself. That way, I'd have real money to justify my fictitious inheritance,' she explained.

I asked, 'Could this child you're carrying be his?'

She denied this possibility vehemently, saying that she'd always been careful when sleeping with him, but it was obvious she was lying … How do I know? Well, for what other reason would she have considered an abortion? She had listed her reasons when I'd posed the hypothesis. But none of them were convincing, you must agree.

A funny thought struck me at that moment: it was all the fault of free initiative. The former employees who wanted to open their own cake shop, my wife who wanted her own catering service — if it weren't for all this entrepreneurialism, none of it might have happened. I left my wife at the breakfast table, and went back into the study to think about what to do.

## 28

I had a few options. I could leave my wife and disappear off the face of the Earth. I could pardon her, and demand that she have an abortion and that she never see my father again, as long as she was married to me. I could hire an assassin to kill my father, as he had set out to do with his former employees, or … I could kill him myself. You may find it odd that a guy who'd been so placid until now could conceive of committing murder; but in the midst of everything that was going on, it really was the most appropriate choice.

I didn't kill him out of revenge, believe me. It was to eliminate an anomaly that, from a young age, had made my life a living hell. My father had tortured me as a child, he'd abandoned me after my mother's death, he'd seduced my wife and then forced her to keep having sex with him and, last but not least, he'd usurped my role as father, by getting her pregnant. Where was the meaning in all this? It took me a while to find the answer, but I did: here was a man who was unable to distinguish between his own desire and reality—hence the anomaly. He didn't think about the consequences of his actions. If something gave him pleasure, he did it, without moral or emotional reservations. This was the main explanation for the sadistic way in which he had treated me. He'd saved me when I was a child only because he'd seen in his own son a way to vent his base instincts. Do you know what else? I cannot say for sure that I was lying when I told the story of the monster who crept into my bed when I was a child …

There, in the study, I also thought about my mother. How could she have fallen in love with such a man? Was it possible he'd managed to hide his true essence from her? No, my mother had most likely glimpsed the monster in him, but had believed that her love could redeem him. 'The love that moves the sun and the other stars.' Dante's line illuminated me. Yes, redemption was possible. But not redemption through Good—this possibility had been lost to me a long time before, with the death of my mother and her love that moved the sun and the other stars. The path to redemption was now one of moral homeopathy. *Similia similibus curantur*—like things are cured by like. Evil, that is. I was no longer interested in how Evil is born in people. For me, at this moment, knowing it was the best alternative was enough.

Yes, you're right. I need to explicitly admit that I believe in God, instead of using subterfuges. But the only God I'm able to believe in is forged in my own likeness and image: the creator not of Heaven or Earth, but of Hell, and Purgatory, to which I descended to redeem my father and myself.

Of course, this has nothing to do with being a man of spirit. You asked me a while back if I thought I was a man of spirit. No, I'm not—which doesn't mean I disagree with the notion that such men are the motors of history. It's just that I've learned that philosophical systems, which serve above all to explain our actions, are not mutually exclusive, as most philosophers believe. What I mean is that I'm not a man of spirit, but I believe that subjectivity is truth. That's from Kierkegaard. And a person's truth is proportional to how much they are willing to risk, based on their faith in God. It must be a lot in my case, judging from what I have at stake.

The remedy I'd use on my father was, in fact, a wish come true. The principle might be homeopathic, but not the dose. I'd wanted to kill him countless times, but now I'd really do it, and with my own hands. Making him a victim would be a way to free him of his own monstrosity, to absolve him — and, thus, to celebrate him as a father. Isn't satisfaction the end of desire? But his redemption couldn't mean my moral damnation, seeing that I didn't want to take my father's place, but surpass him. After hours of anguish, I made another decision: I would have to inflict some kind of pain upon myself that would be a scourge on me until the day I died. Purgatory in life.

Once the general resolutions had been established, I wrote my wife a letter. In it, I advised her to hire a good lawyer to look after her interests. Then she should return to France and have her child there. Full stop. No accusations or goodbyes. My advice was followed to a T. She now lives with the child (a boy) in Paris, together with that American guy she'd dated before she met me. Lucky guy.

I left the letter in my desk drawer, printed a copy of *Future*, put it in a cardboard folder, and erased the file from my computer. It was already night when I left my house for the last time, taking only my unfinished book. There were other things to be done before my father got back from his trip.

## 29

The day I killed my father was a bright day, although the light was hazy, without shadows or contours. Or perhaps it was grey, that shade of grey which even tinges souls that are not usually inclined to melancholy... That would make a good start for a book, wouldn't it? Except that books no longer exist for me.

It was with a blow to the back of his neck and another to the top of his head. But I wasn't alone when I called the police. Through the guy who'd blackmailed my father's driver, I'd spent a small fortune hiring three criminals to come into the house after I'd murdered him. I'd instructed them to immobilise me immediately after the phone-call, even if I changed my mind at the last minute—which I didn't.

'Come and arrest me. I've killed my father,' I said, and hung up the phone. The criminals then did what had been arranged. Two of them held me by the arms and head. Immobilised on an armchair, I could still see my father's body lying on the sofa, before the third crook poured acid into my eyes.

And then the light went out.

This silence ... Are you still there?